WHEN SULLIVAN SAW RED,
IT MEANT BLOOD

Sullivan was annoyed. The Arab terrorist who blocked his path was costing him time and energy he couldn't afford.

The annoyance became anger, the blood lust that made impossible feats possible. Sullivan forgot about the 100-pound backpack he was carrying. It was a soap bubble now. He turned, bent, snatched up the barbed metal mace he had constructed, and whipped it around. It caught the Arab—who was coming at him with a drawn knife—full in the face.

The barbs dug in and ripped, pulling most of his face off. Bits of skull showed through the gory mask where his nose and lips had been. Sullivan struck with the mace again, slashing its bristling killing end into the terrorist's throat, raking it out like an overcooked chicken. Blood spurted, the man pitched over, and just as Sullivan turned away, three more terrorists lunged at him from separate directions, all armed with spiked clubs. . . .

SULLIVAN'S REVENGE

THE #3
SPECIALIST
SULLIVAN'S REVENGE
John Cutter

A SIGNET BOOK
NEW AMERICAN LIBRARY

PUBLISHED BY
THE NEW AMERICAN LIBRARY
OF CANADA LIMITED

PUBLISHER'S NOTE

This novel is a work of fiction. Names, characters, places, and incidents either are the product of the author's imagination or are used fictitiously, and any resemblance to actual persons, living or dead, events, or locales is entirely coincidental.

Copyright © 1984 by John Cutter

First Printing, June, 1984

2 3 4 5 6 7 8 9

SIGNET TRADEMARK REG. U.S. PAT. OFF. AND FOREIGN COUNTRIES
REGISTERED TRADEMARK — MARCA REGISTRADA
HECHO EN WINNIPEG, CANADA

SIGNET, SIGNET CLASSIC, MENTOR, PLUME, MERIDIAN
and NAL BOOKS are published in Canada by The New American
Library of Canada, Limited, Scarborough, Ontario.

PRINTED IN CANADA
COVER PRINTED IN U.S.A.

Prologue: The Specialist

Jack Sullivan stepped off the plane in Portland wearing a light blue suit and carrying a canvas traveling bag. He was brawny but moved fluidly, was mature but buoyant as any twenty-year-old, his thick black hair streaked at the temples with white. He might have passed for a successful salesman of bodybuilding gear, or maybe a rep for a health-spa franchise—until you looked him in the face.

Men who looked in that face, might shiver and move out of his way. It wasn't that the face was hostile or cruel, but there was danger impregnated in it, a glimpse of war experience in the eyes. And scars. The long blue one on the right cheek clearly marked the nick of a bullet.

Women who looked in that face reacted in various ways. If they liked strong, dangerous men, they might shiver, too. An anticipatory shiver that ran down to tingle between their legs. The scars? They weren't disfiguring—and they hinted at an interesting life.

The big man with the small case went to the airport restaurant and ordered eggs, hash browns, and coffee. He glanced at the wall clock. Ten A.M. With luck, he could rent a car by eleven and be on his way out into the mountains.

He hadn't slept much on the plane. He'd been thinking about the mission, wondering if he were on a wild-goose chase. But there was no question of sleeping in a motel now. He wouldn't sleep till he'd come within striking range of the enemy. And then he'd get one good night's sleep, in preparation.

He sipped the black coffee, and his face hardened. His eyes glinted beneath his shaggy brows as he remembered the death that had brought him here. He'd been taking a break between mercenary missions—just after that Lebanese hit for Israeli intelligence—and he and Lily had gone for a cruise off the southern coast of France. He'd gone swimming after they'd anchored near that deserted atoll, and she'd stayed behind on the deck of his cabin cruiser to sunbathe. Now and then he'd surface and see her watching him, her blond head on her crossed arms, and she'd wave lazily. Then he'd decided to swim back to her, and . . . The cabin cruiser had blown up.

The ceramic cup of coffee exploded in Sullivan's hand. He stared at it—there were broken white fragments stuck in his palm, and coffee all over the table. He realized he'd broken it himself, unconsciously crushing it with the pain of remembering.

He tipped the waiter who cleaned up the mess, then spread the map of Oregon out on the table.

There it was—the town where he'd begin his search. It was just about at the center of the long, winding snake of the Rogue River—Sullivan had had a tip that the organization who'd planted that murderous explosive on his boat was hidden away somewhere in the wilds along the Rogue River, in central Oregon. So he'd decided to start the hunt at the center of the river's length, at a little town called Jasper.

6

1
A Warm Western Welcome

As soon as Dave the Dentist walked in with Arn and Lon, Snag knew there'd be trouble in the bar that night. Big trouble.

Sometimes these three came into the Elkhorn Bar and Grill one at a time, or in twos, and there might be trouble then too, but nothing bad. But when all three came together, with Dave Moran leading them, that meant something ugly was cooking.

And Snag didn't like the way Dave was looking at him and Red Eagle.

Red Eagle was three-fourths Indian, and Snag was half. Red lived in Portland, where he declaimed poetry at readings and taught a class on Indian culture. He liked to show off his heritage in the way he dressed: buckskins, feathers, beads. Out here near the reservation, though, there were people like Dave Moran who preferred Indians to keep a low profile.

To be perfectly accurate, Moran and his kind preferred Indians out of the territory entirely. Or dead. "He's revived the local KKK, is what I heard," Snag said. "Blacks, Indians, Mexicans—hell, I think they probably don't even approve of *movies* in color!"

Red Eagle laughed nervously. "Got to be black and white movies, huh? Or just white." He took a pull on his beer and glanced nervously at the three men glaring at them from the bar.

It was an old-fashioned western-mountain-state bar, the walls covered in knotty dark wood, a collection of elaborate beer signs over the door, steer horns and elk horns mounted on each wall making it look as if the walls were challenging one another to a fight. The place was cool and dim; the juke box played a song called *You're the Reason Our Kids are Ugly* . . .

"That one there," Snag said, nodding toward Moran, "they call Dave the Dentist." Moran was a squarish, bristly, prematurely balding man in his early thirties, his thick-fingered hands perpetually grimed from grease; he was a garage mechanic. One of his eyes was Popeye-squinted, and his mustache always had a few crumbs of food clinging to it—or, like now, beer foam. He was drinking boilermakers, whiskey mixed with beer. "You know why they call him Dave the Dentist? Because he holds 'em down, him and his friends of course, and pulls out their teeth with a pair o' pliers."

"Who? Why?"

"Who? Indians. Why? Because he's a sadistic racist asshole." Snag was careful to whisper all of this.

"You think they noticed us?" Red Eagle asked uneasily.

"Sure, man! We're gonna have a helluva fight tonight. Better get drunk first. Hey, Joe . . ." He turned to signal the bartender. "Can we get another pitcher over here?"

He turned back—and blinked. Red Eagle was gone. The side door out of the bar was still half-open. Moran and his friends were laughing.

Snag shrugged and laughed back at them. Showing all those fearless white teeth to Dave the Dentist.

The rednecks stared at him in a way that told

him they intended to make him regret he'd ever been born.

Snag was ready for it. He knew they'd probably kill him—and he didn't give a damn. At least he'd go out that way, in a fight. At least he wouldn't drink himself to death, like a lot of Viet vets. At thirty-eight, he had come to the conclusion that he was an alien in his own culture. He was a double alien, because he was not only part of that great unwanted, best-forgotten breed, the Vietnam veteran, he was also an Indian. He'd felt empty and aimless after the war ended and the Veterans Administration hadn't done much to help him adjust. That's when the drinking started. Now he was just another drunk half-breed. . . .

Better to die kicking a redneck's ass than drunk in a gutter.

Moran set his mug on the bar in a purposeful way that told Snag he was about to get a visit from the local KKK.

And that's when the strangers came in. When Moran got a look at them, he forgot all about Snag.

One of the strangers was coal-black and sported a large gold earring in one ear. The other was as big as a prize bull, but he moved lightly, confidently, but not real cocky. There was something of the Irishman about him—and something intense hidden away in him. That was the way a bomb looked sitting in a B-52: big, cool, hard, and quiet as a park bench—till it exploded. And those scars—that one on his cheek was a bullet graze for sure. A soldier. Professional—maybe a mercenary. Shadows of Vietnam in his eyes.

Snag chuckled, sinking back into his seat. He had a ringside seat for the action—he was sitting with just one booth between his and the corner booth where the strangers had sat down. The

9

barmaid, Angie, insisted on taking their order personally. She smiled like sun on creek water for the brutally good-looking scar-faced one, and he smiled back. There was no trace of a young man's grin in his smile—Snag guessed the stranger knew women almost as well as he knew guns.

Snag couldn't have explained how he was so sure the stranger was a gunman. Snag would have simply shrugged, if you'd asked him, and said, "Twenty years in the service."

The strangers ordered a pitcher of Miller's and sat leaning forward across the wooden table, talking in low voices. Snag couldn't make out most of what they said, but he could tell it wasn't gossip about hunting territory. And it wasn't fag talk—that big black guy wore that earring like a Gypsy would.

"Who the hell let them queers in here?" Moran asked, his voice booming over the Johnny Cash tune now rasping from the jukebox.

Angie tried to shush him. No use. He went right on, his friends laughing, standing at the bar, pretending to stare at the corner booth like a man who's seeing a UFO.

"I said, what the fuck is that *nigger* doing in here!"

"Is that a nigger queer?" Arn asked him rhetorically. "Or a queer nigger?"

"Maybe you oughta ask him, clear it up for the Webster's, Dave," rejoined the other redneck.

"That's a real *perty* earring, little lady!" Dave Moran shouted. "I think that must be Eartha Kitt, Arn!"

The strangers kept right on talking, not so much as glancing toward the bar. They ignored the jeering as if it were the prattling of children on tricycles.

Snag watched Moran—and smiled when he saw

10

Moran reacting to the strangers' indifference to him. He turned red, and seemed uncertain of himself. Because it was obvious the strangers weren't scared of Moran in the least. And even Moran knew there might be a good reason for that.

Moran might have shrugged it off and turned away, the whole thing might not have happened—except that Arn kept egging him on. And that big-busted redhead from the hunting lodge came in. Moran wanted her, and he was one of those fools who think women are impressed by bullies.

So Dave-the-Dentist Moran turned to the bar, knocked back a boilermaker in three gulps, and then turned toward the strangers. He seemed to gather his balls up into his spine, and crossed the room to the strangers' table, taking care to swagger.

He stood over the table, breathing out fumes Snag could smell six feet away.

The scar-faced stranger sat facing Snag. A flicker of irritation passed over his face. That was all.

Snag was a little worried for the stranger. It wouldn't be smart to underestimate Moran. Dave the Dentist had been in a lot of fights. And he was strong as a bulldozer.

The jukebox ran out of songs; the bar was quiet, as everyone listened, watched, waited.

"This ain't a gay bar, girls," Moran said.

Snag could see the scar-faced stranger was still hoping Moran would go away. Probably he didn't want a fight that would attract the sheriff. He was a man bent on business, and he didn't want to call attention to himself.

But Arn and a few of the others took the strangers' lack of reaction for cowardice. There were hoots from various corners of the room, and shouts of encouragement to Moran.

11

"Queers is bad enough," Moran persisted, "but niggers is even worse."

"Actually," the black man said with a trace of a foreign accent, "I believe that in proper grammar that should be 'niggers *are* even worse,' because 'niggers' is plural."

The scar-faced man laughed. "Malta," he said, addressing the black, "did you set this up? Is this one of your little jokes? Because if it is—"

"But no, my friend! I promised no more practical jokes!"

Sullivan shrugged. He turned to Moran. "In that case, friend, it wouldn't amuse my friend much if I were to kill you. He's not in one of his humorous moods. So you can go back to your high chair at the bar with your head still sitting on your shoulders."

Yowls of delight came from every corner of the Elkhorn. The big-busted redhead was laughing out loud.

Moran clenched his fists. But he didn't use them. Instead, he made a long snorting sound and then spat into the strangers' beer pitcher.

A yellow oyster of spittle floated in the beer foam. Snag held his breath.

Jack Sullivan sighed, and stared thoughtfully at the beer. "I can't lose my temper because you called me 'nigger lover,' because it's no insult to be called a friend to a black man. As for 'faggot'—only people who're scared they might be homosexual get shook up by that one. But the beer—you've ruined my beer, man. And I was *thirsty*. So I guess I'm going to have to drink your blood."

On the word "blood" he slammed his elbow sideways into Moran's groin.

Sullivan moved into a secondary strike position as Moran doubled over, swearing, clutching his crushed balls.

Swiveling in the booth, knees drawn up, leaning back on the wooden bench, bracing: Sullivan did it all in less than a second, while Moran was still bent over. And then he kicked upward like a Russian dancer, the toe of his right boot connecting with Moran's teeth. Moran went over backward as if he were trying to impress the redhead with a back flip. He ended up rocking on his ass, one hand covering his mouth, the other cupping his groin. Blood gushed dark red through his fingers, carrying bits of broken teeth with it.

Arn shouted, "That's chickenshit fighting! You ain't gonna catch me like that!" And he roared across the room, a beer bottle in his hand like a belaying pin.

Sullivan simply stood, blanking his face, loose-limbed and calm, waiting for Arn to come into reach. He blocked the down-swinging beer bottle with his left arm, and put the whole weight of his massive upper body into a right to the point of Arn's jaw. The redneck spun and fell heavily against a table, which folded under him like a cardboard box, broken beer pitchers spilling yellow foam and shattered glass to either side.

Sullivan didn't stop to contemplate his victory; there was no time for gloating. Chunky, long-blond-haired Lon was coming at him, grinning, sure he'd caught Sullivan off guard. Lon came low, in a football player's tackle. Sullivan braced and grunted as Lon plowed his right shoulder into Sullivan's midriff. Lon had picked up momentum charging across the room, and he succeeded in driving Sullivan back against the divider between two booths with a force that made the tables shiver.

Lon kept pinning him against the divider with

his right shoulder, his left arm cocking for a gut punch.

The punch never landed. Sullivan made cups of his hands and clapped them expertly over Lon's ears. Hard. Lon screamed as the brutal hammer of sudden air pressure smashed into his eardrums. He clapped his hands to his head in reflex, still bent over in the tackler's crouch. Sullivan brought his knee up with machine precision and hydraulic force, and everyone watching jerked his or her head in sympathy at hearing the crack of Sullivan's knee-cap on Lon's jaw. Lon jerked back, poleaxed, and fell on his side, out cold.

There was one more—a lumberjack, still wearing his yellow hard hat. He was an unknown quantity, stepping into the fight probably for the same reason Moran had—he had his eye on that redhead. He had shoulders like the Rockies under a red plaid shirt, and most of his face was beard. He might've been harder for Sullivan—only the guy never finished his rush.

Malta—the one a witness would later describe as "a sort of black Mr. Clean"—stepped in, moving like a matador to distract the lumberjack from Sullivan. The hardhat swerved, swinging at this new target; Malta ducked and jabbed with his hand twisted into a Nukite palm strike at the base of the lumberjack's skull. Malta didn't seem to hit the man very hard—but his victim fell like one of the trees that he assassinated for the paper companies, his hard hat coming off to roll on end like a coin.

There was a moment of silence as the stunned bar patrons looked at the four felled rednecks and tried to come to terms with the suddenness of it all. The fight had lasted about a minute and a half. Normally a bar brawl went on for a half-hour or more and ended either messily or inconclusively.

Malta, sighing, wiping his hand on a napkin, said, "I do *so* dislike having to participate in this sort of thing."

Sullivan laughed and went to the bartender. "You explain to any local law that—"

" 'S okay," the bartender interrupted. "They jumped you. I saw it."

Sullivan laid two one-hundred-dollar bills on the bar. "For the damage."

He and Malta headed for the door.

Sullivan's heart was still pumping with adrenaline as he trudged beside Malta across the parking lot outside the Elkhorn. But he felt no pleasure in triumph. They hadn't been pros. The real fight was still ahead, a fight with real pros—and one he stood a good chance of losing. But that didn't matter. At the very least he'd take some of the terrorists down with him, because the bottom line was: *He wanted their blood.*

By accident or design, they'd murdered Lily. His white-skinned Lily, Lily the eternal innocent. They'd not only taken from him the only woman he'd ever felt really close to, they'd taken something precious from the world. Because that woman had *cared* about people. And there weren't many like that left.

Yeah, he'd make 'em pay.

The autumn night was misty but gentle. They could hear the river swishing and gurgling beyond the strip of trees between the bar and the boulder-strewn bank. Here the river was comparatively easygoing, like an African predator with its belly full, temporarily placid. A half-mile farther on it once more took up its tortuous twisting and white-water rushing, earning its name, Rogue.

They'd just reached the gravel edging the highway when they heard running bootsteps behind them. More trouble?

Sullivan spun, crouching.

A short, stocky, dark-skinned man with high cheekbones stood there looking from one to the other. He wore jeans and an old army jacket, the insignia stripped off it.

Sullivan waited for him to make a move. The man's face was grim, determined. And then it broke into a smile. "Came to welcome you to Jasper," he said. There was friendly irony in his voice. He extended his hand. "People call me Snag."

Sullivan straightened and shook the Indian's hand. It was a rough hand, hardened by a life spent working outdoors. Standing closer, Sullivan could see that Snag was in his late thirties. There was a scar along his scalp that looked like a shrapnel track. Probably a vet. Sullivan could also see that he was moderately drunk.

"Thanks," Sullivan said. "Thank your friends for the 'warm western welcome.'"

"They ain't no friends of mine, mister." Sullivan could see him clearly in the light from one of the town's two streetlights; the light was directly overhead on a tarred wooden pole. The Indian went on, "That was a fine demonstration of hand-to-hand. I was an instructor in that once. . . ." His voice was a little wistful. He turned to Malta. "But I never saw that chop you used before. That was something. You give lessons?"

Malta shook his head. "I prefer that the rest of the world remain at a disadvantage to me."

Snag chuckled. "Now, listen, I know I look a little drunk. Maybe you got me pegged for a drunk Indian. Maybe I am. But I don't have to be—not when I got some work I like doin'. I figure you guys are out here for business. Like maybe you need a guide— you looking for land out here?"

Sullivan shook his head. "Not for land. Anyway, I don't think we'll be hiring anyone to—"

16

"Look . . ." Snag raised both his fists. Not in a threatening gesture, but one that signified determination and strength. "I can do anything you need. I ain't lookin' for a handout. Just a job. I'll work for anything—I want to work with you guys. When I was in Nam there were guys who . . ." He broke off, looking disgusted. "I must be going to hell, all right. Falling into that 'when-I-was-in-Nam' trip."

"I know what you mean," Sullivan said slowly. "Putting it all on the line with guys you can trust. There's no feeling like it. . . . You know these hills?"

"Every goddamn rock."

Sullivan looked into Snag's eyes. And knew he could trust him. He had fought beside such men. He surprised Malta by giving Snag his real name. "My name's Jack Sullivan."

Malta shrugged. "Since we are indiscreetly passing our real names about, mine is Malta."

"We're staying at the Riverbend Motel," Sullivan said. "You want to walk us down, we'll talk."

. "Yeah. You bet." Snag showed no eagerness; it was clear he was holding back. He walked a little too carefully as he fell in step beside them, like a man who's trying not to show he's drunk.

They walked along the deserted highway, away from the cone of light, into the pine-scented shadow beneath the trees flanking the road. A semitruck hauling logs rumbled by, shedding bits of bark in its windy wake. That was all.

"We're looking for a 'survivalist training center,' " Sullivan began. "It's along the Rogue River somewhere. That's pretty much all we know about it." He hesitated, wondering if he should tell Snag the whole story. He trusted him instinctively, but information could be dangerous to people. And Malta wouldn't approve of telling so much about their mission—a highly illegal mission—to a complete

17

stranger. But Sullivan had learned to trust his instincts, his hunches. They had carried him through a decade of firefights. And anyway, if the man was going to guide them—they'd need a guide—he had a right to know the truth. Just going into the target area could be lethal.

Snag was saying, "Survivalists—that's people who think a nuclear war is coming, right? And they go off into the countryside for survival training to get ready for the end of civilization."

"That's right. It involves paramilitary training. So anyone who stumbles on such a place isn't surprised to see survivalists dressed in combat clothes, carrying weapons. . . . That makes a 'survivalist training camp' a good cover." He decided to trust his instincts. He would tell Snag the rest.

In Nam, the CIA had sometimes come and asked him to evaluate a defector—more often than not, a supposed defector was actually a communist agent posing as a defector to effect a "misinformation" mission. Sullivan had always known which was which, within minutes. Some claimed he was telepathic. But that wasn't it. He simply had a talent for looking deep into the men he met. So Sullivan said:

"We've heard stories that there's a training camp for terrorists hidden somewhere along the Rogue River. It's disguised as a 'survivalist' training center. I have reason to believe that the man who runs that camp ordered a hit on me. My woman was killed . . . maybe they intended to kill me instead, maybe not. I don't care. I'm here to find 'em—and make 'em pay for that. And to put a stop to what they're up to."

"Just you?" There was no disrespect in Snag's voice. Only worry.

"Me and a few friends. I've sent for help."

"I understand why you want to get at them, man. But maybe you should let the law do your revenging for you. There's bound to be a lot of them."

Sullivan shook his head. "I'm afraid they'd slip away if the law was coming at them. Or they'd fake 'em out, convince the law they were real survivalists. They'd slip through the noose. The law's noose. They won't slip through mine. I don't expect you to take up the fight with me—just guide me. But that could be dangerous too."

"If what you say about these people is true," Snag said grimly, "just give me a rifle and I'll back you up." He added, "I don't know about a 'survivalist' camp, but my Uncle Blue Bear claimed he saw some soldiers on the river about eight miles up— that was back in August. Said they looked like a funny mix of foreigners."

Sullivan and Malta exchanged looks. "That might be it," Sullivan said. "Can you get us there?"

"Sure. Rough country. But sure. Take us a day or three. I can take you partway in my Jeep. The rest on foot."

They'd reached the motel. They stood in the dim yellow light under the guttering Riverbend Motel sign and shook hands all around once more.

"Seven tomorrow morning," Sullivan said. "I'll be in cabin twelve. We'll be ready. I guess I don't need to tell you—"

"I know, man: no booze. Not even a beer. You got supplies?"

Sullivan and Malta looked embarrassedly at each other. "Supplies? Uh . . . backpacks. Guns. Ammo. Not much else."

"No sweat. I can get what we need."

"We haven't talked about money."

"Just pay my expenses and minimum wage. . . .

19

I've been waiting years to see Dave the Dentist get his."

"The hell. Two hundred a day plus expenses."

Snag's eyes widened. "On the level?"

"Plus a bonus if we find the place."

"I'll take you to hell and back for that."

Sullivan smiled sadly. "That's what I figure you'll have to do."

Snag grinned. "I been there before." He nodded and walked back toward the Elkhorn, where his Jeep was parked.

Sullivan and Malta watched him go. Malta asked, "Can we trust him? You told him a great deal, Jack."

"I know. We can. Come on." They turned to walk across the asphalt parking lot to the cabins arranged in a semicircle behind the darkened motel's office.

A swath of light whipped across the tarmac in front of them—the headlights of a big camper's van. The van jounced up the driveway and jerked to a halt in front of them, cutting off their access to the cabins. The man sitting in the passenger side up front was carrying a shotgun. And that shotgun was resting on the frame of the van door's open window. Pointing out at them. The van's cab light came on, and Dave the Dentist grinned bloodily at them above the shotgun in his white-knuckled hands.

20

2
The Scenic
Route to Death

"Always complications." Sullivan sighed.

"That what you think it is? A complication?" Moran asked. "Bullshit. Gonna be a lot more'n that for you, asshole. You're gonna *pay*."

Lon and Arn had gotten out of the van at the rear, were flanking Malta and Sullivan with rifles in their hands, two 30.06's ready to fire from the hip.

Sullivan glanced over his shoulder at the motel's small office outbuilding. It was dark; the manager was asleep.

"Ain't nobody gonna help you, motherfucker," Lon said, raising the gun as if to use its barrel as a club.

"Hold it, now," Moran commanded. "Don't get that close to these two kung-fu hotshots. We'll do it with guns from a safe distance."

Lon backed off. "Okay. Get in the fucking van, nigger. You too, faggot." Arn opened the side door of the big van, behind Moran.

Sullivan made an internal effort and managed to control his temper. If he made a move, Moran would let him have it. He and Malta were unarmed. It looked bad. But these were amateurs—they'd make a mistake. He hoped.

Malta sighed and shrugged, then climbed into the van. The lumberjack, Sullivan saw as he climbed in after Malta, was at the wheel. Moran had twisted around in his seat to keep them covered till Arn and Lon could get in at the rear. "Close the side door," Moran ordered. Malta was nearest the door; he closed it. The lumberjack put the van into gear as Lon and Arn got in at the back, slamming the rear door and taking up seats at the back on two closed beer coolers, rifles in hand. They kept the rear interior light on. The cab light went out as the van lurched ahead, swung toward the drive and out onto the highway.

Lon and Arn sat glaring at them; every so often Lon reached up to massage the swollen place on his jaw where Sullivan had knocked him out.

Sullivan and Malta sat on either side of the engine casing—it was a flat-nosed van, the engine between and back of the front seats. They sat in small extra-passenger seats back-to-back with Moran and the lumberjack. Moran sat half-turned in his seat, behind Malta. He had the shotgun pointed at the ceiling now, Sullivan noted; the seat back was too high to make it possible for him to keep the shotgun trained on them from the front. He'd have to get up out of his seat and prop the gun beside the headrest. That would take a few seconds.

But Lon and Arn had clear shots at them. And they didn't take their eyes off. Once Arn said, "Oh, the things we gonna do to you. Oh, the things we gonna do. Oh, man." And then he smiled in twisted anticipation.

Malta replied, "Don't forget to crush my testicles in a vise. That's my favorite."

Sullivan laughed, until Moran reached back and hit them each glancingly on the side of the head with the muzzle of the twelve-gauge.

It didn't do much damage, that glancing blow, but it stung like the devil. Worse, it was humiliating.

Sullivan had to work hard to keep from jumping

22

Moran then. Not yet, he told himself. The moment will come.

Sullivan looked over his shoulder at the road outside the windshield. Insects flared like the eyes of ghosts in the headlights; the van took a curve and for a moment the headlights cut out into empty space over the cliff edge. They were high up in the hills.

"We almost there," the lumberjack said. "This place is perfect. Ain't no one there. And I know where they left the chain saws locked up."

Malta was sitting by the door. Impossible to say what the roadside was like beyond that door. If they went out it, they might go over a cliff.

Chain saws . . .

In metal brackets on the rear of the blocky, rumbling upthrust of the engine casing, between Sullivan and Malta, was a gasoline can. The top wasn't securely closed on the can, and when the van jounced, a little gasoline would slosh out onto the can's top. Enough.

By the sound of the sloshing in the can, it was about three-fourths full. It was a big risk . . . but it was the only chance.

Malta glanced at the sliding door in the vibrating metal wall beside him.

"You can stop looking at that door, nigger," one of the rednecks told Malta. "Before you'd get through it, I'd put a bullet in you in a place that'd hurt real bad."

"Okay if I have a last cigarette?" Sullivan asked, looking resigned to death.

"Sure, boy," Moran said, "an' you better enjoy it." Moran looked toward the front, asking the lumberjack, "Where the hell is that turnoff?"

Sullivan took out his lighter and puffed a Lucky Strike alight. He noted that Arn and Lon had looked

23

away for a moment, craning to see out the front window.

Sullivan bent and whispered to Malta, "Get ready to open the door."

Malta looked at him in alarm.

Sullivan straightened, drew a lungful of smoke, and then tossed the still-glowing butt at the top of the gas can.

Flames leaped up instantly, yellow edged with blue, eating toward the cap of the gas can.

Arn jerked to his feet, gaping at the gas can, shrieking, "Damn you, fool, you're gonna . . ."

He broke off as Lon, grabbing up an open sleeping bag and dropping his rifle in a hysterical response to the emergency, pushed past him to get at the flames, hoping to damp down the fire before the can blew.

Sullivan was following Malta out the side door. Moran turned in his seat as he went by, but he had no hope of getting a shot at them from that angle.

And Sullivan dived headfirst into the night.

He had a blurred impression of the earth whirling at him, and then, in reflex, he tucked his right shoulder under him and went limp. He hit, and rolled, desperately scrabbling to stop himself, to keep from rolling off a cliffside. But he came safely to a halt on his back; the van had slowed for a curve and the road shoulder here was soft with the fallen needles of overleaning pines.

He lay for a moment on his back, getting his breath, and then sat up—just in time to see the van, filled with flame so it overflowed from the windows, careening off the edge of a cliff, the men inside shrieking on the way down. He heard the *crunch-creak-thud* as the van exploded somewhere below.

Sullivan and Malta got to their feet. Sullivan's

shoulder throbbed but seemed unbroken. "You okay, Malta?"

"Yes . . . yes, Jack. I'm okay. A few bruises." He was almost invisible in the darkness of the mountain road. "You?"

"I'm fine. Except . . ." He crumpled the cigarette pack still clutched in his hand. "Except I'm out of cigarettes."

There was a subdued crackle of dying flames from the wreck below the lip of the cliff. Sullivan and Malta had trudged away down the road. So they didn't see the silhouette of a man's head rising above the edge of the cliff near the rutted place where the van had gone over. They didn't see the man pull himself wearily onto the lip of rock and then reach down to help another man climb up beside him. Dave the Dentist and the lumberjack. The lumberjack had a broken arm. Dave Moran had two broken ribs, a broken nose, and a couple of broken fingers. Both men had jumped from the van just as it had gone over; they'd fallen, flailing, on the shelf of rock jutting just below the cliff's edge. Moran had lain unconscious for a while . . .

They were better off, Moran had to admit to himself, than Arn and Lon, crushed and burned up in the fire.

Moran forced himself to his feet, and helped the lumberjack—Bud Hauser—to stand beside him. They staggered off down the road.

A semi driven by a friend of Hauser's gave them a ride a few minutes later. They made up a story to tell.

They didn't want the sheriff in on this. They wanted the big mick and the nigger to themselves. When the time was right.

25

Sullivan and Malta were footsore from the four-mile walk back to the motel, and aching from a dozen bruises apiece. But there was no rest quite yet. There were two more dangerous men waiting for them at the Riverbend.

The men got out of a blue Ford sedan when they saw Sullivan and Malta arriving.

Sullivan shook their hands. "Good to see you grunts again. Let's go into my place, polish off a bottle of Johnnie Walker Black Label. I'll give you a general briefing; we'll go into details tomorrow."

The four men went into Sullivan's cabin. The two new men sat on the bed; Malta sprawled with a sigh in an armchair in the opposite corner. Sullivan poured out the drinks and sat on a coffee table.

For a moment they sipped in silence; Sullivan looked at the two men, reassessing them. They hadn't changed much.

The bigger one was Bruno Rolff. He was a solidly built West German who was blond when he let his hair grow out enough. Usually he kept it pig-shaved. He had a genuine Heidelberg scar on his cheek; thick, humorless lips; and small blue eyes like chips of ice. He seemed compact, contained within himself, placid.

Johnny Merlin, by contrast, was gangly and nervous, "a specialist with wires and a wired specialist." One of his knees was always bouncing like the stick shift over the vibrating engine of a dragster; hold that knee down, and the other one would start bouncing. His big, heavily veined hands were forever busy: leave a pen and paper near them, and he'd start doodling; leave a pack of cards near him, and he'd automatically start doing card tricks. He had shoulder-length brown hair tied back, and a small goatee. His long, gaunt face was like an old-fashioned portrait of the devil. But there was no one more loyal, no one more reliable.

Both men wore inconspicuous civvies; Merlin wore threadbare jeans and a workshirt, rotting tennis shoes; Rolff wore neatly pressed denims.

Rolff was a bush-kill specialist. Merlin was an accomplished sniper and explosives man. Both men were all-around fighters; both had fought beside Sullivan on mercenary missions in North Africa. Merlin had worked with Sullivan in Nam. Malta had recruited them for Sullivan, and arranged the meeting. That was Malta's specialty: personnel, supplies, intelligence.

Before now, Malta had recruited Sullivan's services for other people; he had found people who had a just cause that involved a mission of vengeance. Sullivan was paid to be the avenger. But this time Sullivan had gone to Malta and hired him, asking him to recruit two more men—for his personal mission of vengeance.

Merlin couldn't contain himself any longer. "So what's the scam?"

Sullivan smiled. Both men, it was clear, were eager to work. Merlin, especially—he was one of those men who'd come back from Vietnam and had instantly felt lost on his own home soil. He lived for combat, for the thrill of Russian roulette. Because every professional fighting man knew that sooner or later, if you kept looking for action, you'd find a bullet.

Sullivan gave them the lowdown he'd given Snag. Then he said, "I won't bullshit you—the odds are long against us. We're up against pros. It couldn't be much worse."

"Yes it could," Merlin said. "It could turn out the training camp's a myth, and there's no job at all. The way I feel, no job is worse than a bad job."

Sullivan chuckled. "I remember that day in Nam. I had a suicide mission. I went to the platoon and asked for volunteers . . ."

"You said, 'I need some fools!' "

"And you said, 'That's me!' "

They laughed, and Sullivan said, "This mission's just as foolish. But I'm paying a five-thousand-dollar advance per man—guaranteed even if the mission is called off—and then thirty thousand more apiece if we go into action."

Rolff shrugged. "For how long?"

"Should be all over—one way or the other—inside a month."

Merlin looked impressed. "That's a lot of money for a few weeks' work."

"You'd better understand," Sullivan said, "this is illegal in a big way. Won't make any difference to the cops if we're snuffing terrorists. Vigilantism is against the law. And the weapons we'll be using are outlawed."

Merlin shrugged. "I'm willing to risk it."

"Me too," Rolff said. "What weapons?"

"Your specialties, and more. Malta's a good provider."

"But not much for the graveyard shift—he's asleep!" Merlin remarked.

Malta was slumped in his chair, snoring.

"He earned it tonight," Sullivan said. "We had some trouble." Sullivan poured them another drink and told them about Dave the Dentist.

"Always complications," Merlin said, chuckling.

They were up at six-thirty, breakfast eaten by seven-fifteen, and by seven-thirty they were gathered around the table in Sullivan's cabin, drinking coffee and going over a topographical map of the area. The Rogue twisted viciously through hills and

28

canyons, with few straight stretches. "We're here," Snag said, tapping the spot marked "Jasper." "The place I figure for the 'proximate location of this camp is up here. . . ." He tapped a spot along the river about twenty miles northeast.

"Not far!" Rolff said, surprised.

"Not as the crow flies. But there's no road for the last twelve miles of it. We'll have to do some hiking. That's some pretty hairy wilderness. Dangerous. Not many hunters or hikers in there. Mostly just a few fur poachers. See this mountain?" He tapped another place just a few miles north of the target area. "Not really a mountain—an overgrown hill. But it's at the foot of Mount Carmen—they say it's still volcanically active. Underground it's connected up with Mount St. Helens. So our little mountain— Mount Chemwa—is a fumarole. A small branch of the bigger volcano. And all up and down its slopes there, it's coming out with hot springs, mud pits, sulfur pits—too unpredictable to be a good tourist area. That's one reason it might be a good area for someone to have an illegal training center—it's dangerous in there, so you don't get many campers. The mud flows are always changing place."

"Seems to me," Merlin remarked, "the USA is a funny place for a terrorist training center. You'd think it would be off in the North African desert, or a jungle . . . or Libya."

"That's how it looks at first glance," Sullivan countered. "But most possible host countries would be paranoid about paramilitary camps they aren't controlling. The USA is liberal enough to let them get away with it under this 'survivalist' cover—this is almost the only country in the world where that survivalist bullshit happens. Of course, the feds would come down hard on the place if they knew about the terrorism connection."

"Just exactly how do they run this training center?" Rolff asked, frowning. He seemed skeptical.

"It's in two sections," Sullivan replied. "One provides men to work anonymously for terrorist operations—for anyone who pays. Say one Arab faction wants a hit against Qaddafi. They might pay the Blue Man to do it; the Blue Man—the terrorist trainers' chief—sends his agents to bomb the Libyan embassies. Then the Arabs who paid for the bombing claim responsibility—from a safe distance. Then maybe Qaddafi would hire the Blue Man to hit the Arab faction that blew up his embassy—not knowing who had really done it. They'll work for anyone who pays. The other section trains terrorists for their own operations. Most terrorists are trained by the Soviet GRU or the KGB. If you don't want the Russians breathing down your neck, if you don't want to be indebted to them, then you go elsewhere to get your men trained. You go to the Blue Man. How they get these men into the country, I don't know."

"There must be more than one nationality taking training at this place," Merlin said. "Some of them would probably be hostile to the other trainees—how do they deal with that?"

"I don't know," Sullivan said. "Most of how this thing works is still a mystery to me. But I'm going to find out as much about it as I can. 'Know thine enemy.' You guys ready to head for the hills?"

"I been ready for months. Let's do it!" Merlin rejoined.

"The weapons," Rolff said tersely.

"They're in that crate. Automatic weapons, explosives—all the best. We'll look them over at the first camp. I'd rather not unpack them here . . . I'm afraid the sheriff might show up anytime to question me about that business with the dead rednecks. If he makes the connection."

Rolff nodded. "We go."

It was a crisp autumn morning. The sun had just topped the pine ridge overlooking the motel to the east. The morning mist curled blue-silver around the gray trunks of the pines lining the road. The big Jeep cut through tenuous scarves of that mist as it swung off the highway and onto the gravel road leading into the hills. Dust mingled with fog behind them.

Snag was at the wheel; Sullivan sat in the bucket seat beside him; Merlin and Rolff sat in the back. Malta was waiting back at the motel. He was their outside-world liaison man. Sullivan had a heavy-duty military radio with which he and Malta would keep in contact.

Sullivan watched a deer bounding across the road ahead of them, but his mind was elsewhere. He was uneasy about the possible aftermath of his destruction of Dave the Dentist and company. The men had had it coming—they'd bragged about murdering Indians, and they would surely have killed Sullivan and Malta. But the local judiciary wouldn't look at it that way. The sheriff's department would probably conclude the men were drunk; one of them got careless with a match and . . .

But someone might have seen them force Malta and Sullivan into the van.

Sullivan glanced at Snag. He hadn't mentioned the rednecks since the night before. Maybe the bodies hadn't been identified yet. "Hey, Snag, you hear anything about those rednecks we dusted at the bar?"

Snag shouted back over the hungry rumble of the engine and the creaking of its springs as it bounced

31

over the rutted road, " 'Bout three inna morning my brother got called out to do some kinda rescue operation. Came back this morning said they were all dead. Burned up. Some folks saw 'em get into that van with the chain-saw jockey. Got all boozed up and went off at the curve." He looked sidelong at Sullivan and grinned. "Maybe."

Sullivan nodded. Snag would've mentioned it if anyone had pointed the finger at Sullivan. Still, if the sheriff persisted in asking questions . . .

The sun rose above the trees, reaching down to burn away the morning mists and heat the canvas top of the Jeep, so that after a while Sullivan rolled down his window for cool air. Scents of fern and wet moss and rotting wood came to him, all mingled with pine sap. They slowed as the road became more twisting, wending through hills; the pine forest was more frequently broken by semiarid patches of scrub and mesquite and Joshua trees growing in ancient lava beds; the long-cold volcanic rock appeared as abrupt swatches of black and blue-gray in the background of greenery.

They were heading roughly northeast, paralleling the course of the Rogue River, which was surging through the trees somewhere to their left, hidden behind folds of volcanic rock.

About one o'clock Sullivan ordered a stop for rations and to give his kidneys a rest—Snag drove with wild abandon, as if the Jeep were an Indian pony galloping across the Great Plains, and it made for a punishing ride on these rough-cut roads.

They stopped beside a log bridge over a creek. They sat in the sun on a fallen tree trunk and ate their sandwiches in thoughtful silence. "Maybe we get a little fresh venison while we're up here," Snag said, peering into the woods. "There's a doe in there . . ."

"Not yet," Sullivan said. "But we can try out the weapons—not on deer, though. Not sporting to use automatic weapons on deer. Except in an emergency. But if you think we're safe out here, Snag, maybe we'll field-test the machine guns."

Snag shrugged. "Safe as anywhere. You can never tell when there might be a ranger around, though. But you got to check out the weapons before we get near the target area."

They finished their meal, and then Sullivan used a crowbar to open the big wooden crate in the back of the Jeep. He selected a pair of M16's, an AK47, an Israeli Uzi machine pistol, an H&K MP5 machine pistol, and an Austrian SSG sniper rifle.

Loaded down with all these weapons of destruction and the ammo, they hiked a short distance into the woods and paused by an outcropping of volcanic rock to set up a target . . .

And two bullets smashed into the trunk of a tree close beside Sullivan's head.

3
Fool's Skirmish

The Specialist's team acted by instinct. All four men threw themselves to the mossy humus and crawled quickly to cover behind a big overgrown fallen log. Snag had carried one of the M16's and ammo. He quickly fed a clip into it and moved in a crouch to the other end of the log. Rolff took the H&K machine pistol and crept around the other way. Sullivan was loading the AK47; Merlin had picked up the sniper's rifle, was fixing the scope onto it.

Sullivan cocked the AK47 and looked cautiously through the vines overtop the yard-thick log between him and the unknown gunman. He expected another burst of gunfire, but there was none. He saw no one in the copse of trees across the fern meadow. Then he heard a crashing to his right; he swung the gun around, tensing to fire—and then relaxed. Just a deer, a big-eyed doe, lifting its white tail as it flashed through the forest.

He jerked back toward the fern meadow, Merlin up beside him now, when he heard the rattle of machine-pistol fire. "Shit!" Sullivan swore.

Because he'd just realized that in all probability the gunshots had been fired by a hunter who'd been aiming at that deer. And if an innocent man had died, Sullivan, and Jack Sullivan alone, would take responsibility.

He leaped up and ran, skirting the log and weaving through the trees at the edge of the meadow.

He pulled up short, and his heart went cold when he saw the man sprawled at Rolff's feet. Rolff was pointing the machine pistol down, apparently about to administer the *coup de grace*.

"Dammit, Rolff, hold it!" Sullivan shouted.

Rolff looked up at Sullivan in surprise. "Hold what?"

The man on the ground looked up at Sullivan too.

Sullivan let out a long breath as he realized that the man hadn't been shot. His hands were behind his head. He'd thrown himself down because Rolff had ordered him to. His deer-hunting rifle lay in the ferns a few feet away.

He wore a red hunter's jacket and baggy khaki trousers; he was a chunky, round-faced man with pudgy fingers that trembled at the back of his neck, and round eyes; he had a scraggly brown beard to which bits of leaves and moss clung now. "Don't shoot! I didn't see you fellas! I was shooting at a deer!"

"What kind of deer?" Sullivan asked.

"A doe! Full grown!"

Sullivan nodded. "I saw it. Okay. Get up." As the man shakily got to his feet, Sullivan turned to Rolff. "That was the Uzi I heard. What for?"

"I fired a burst over his head to warn him, because he ran when he saw me. I thought we'd better question him."

Sullivan sighed. "Next time, you don't go into action unless I tell you. I'm in charge here."

Rolff nodded.

"What's your name?" Sullivan asked the hunter.

"Car ... Carlton. Myron Carlton." He stepped back, startled, as Snag stepped from the brush, M16 in hand.

Sullivan noticed Carlton was staring at the M16 and then at the Uzi.

"CIA special operations exercises," Sullivan told him. "You got a hunting license?"

Carlton nodded more than he had to and fumbled in his coat pocket, finally producing a card. Sullivan pretended to scrutinize it doubtfully. "Okay," he said at last. He handed the card back and looked Carlton in the eyes. "Now, it's gonna be a big temptation to talk about this back at the Elkhorn bar. How you saw the CIA men in the woods with their fancy guns. Well, you can—in six weeks. In six weeks, talk all you want about it. But not till then—we don't want a lot of sightseers out here getting themselves shot. We're testing weapons here, see. . . . If anyone comes around, I'm gonna ask 'em where they heard about it. And I memorized your address from that card. Got it?"

"Yes, sir! You bet! I'm a patriot! I—"

"Okay, okay. Get out of the area. Fast. Take your gun and go."

They watched him scramble away through the brush, and after he was well away, Snag and Sullivan laughed with relief. But Rolff wasn't laughing.

"You should have killed him," Rolff said flatly. "He might bring the law down on us. He noticed the guns."

"I think he bought my story," Sullivan said.

"It would be wiser not to take chances," Rolff said.

"There's more than one kind of wisdom," Jack Sullivan replied.

When they'd reassembled at the testing ground by the volcanic outcropping, Sullivan lit a cigarette and said, "Merlin gets a gold star on his report card today. His mom will be pleased. 'Cause he waited for me to tell him to move out."

Snag looked sheepish; Rolff looked blank. Merlin grinned. And said, "Garsh, thanks, teach."

"Let's test the gear," Sullivan said. "But listen, Snag—check out the M16 and then get up on that crag, stand lookout. I don't want any more 'incidents.'"

For almost two hours the hillside echoed with the cracks and rattles and booms and thuds of the various weapons. Merlin set up pine cones on the outcropping and, with the sniper's rifle, shattered them at centerpoint from up to sixty yards, after resetting the sights. "How's that Uzi feel?" Sullivan asked after Rolff had torn a stump to pieces with it.

"Feather-light," Rolff said. "Good velocity, good close-quarters gun."

Sullivan selected the H&K MP5, a favorite weapon of the U.S. special forces antiterrorist team. The MP5 weighed only 4.4 pounds. It was just 12.8 inches long, and looked roughly like a sawed-off submachine gun. It bucked like a rabid mustang in his hand, but within a thirty-foot range it spread in a reasonably narrow cone-of-fire. Another good close-quarters weapon.

"We'll have to wait on testing the explosives and the bazookas, the mortars—we're too close in to the town for that kind of noise," Sullivan decided.

They returned to the Jeep and packed the equipment in the crate, and soon were jouncing again over the red-clay roads. They'd left the gravel road behind for a forest-service firefighting access road.

About dusk they stopped beside another creek and pulled off the road, driving between the trees till the Jeep was concealed in the brush. They made camp in a hollow on top of a small ridge. From the moment they arrived at the campsite, there was a man on watch at all times, beginning with Snag.

After the tents were pitched, the fire built, water drawn from the crystalline stream twenty feet below them, Merlin took Snag's place on watch, and Snag cooked steaks. It was the only fresh meat they'd brought; after tonight it would all be canned—unless they were lucky with game. But Sullivan had decided that game would have to be shot with the heavy-duty crossbows he'd brought along—he didn't want gunshots to alert the enemy. The enemy might expect hunters to be in the area, but they might also check them out. Sullivan had no doubt that the Blue Man sent out far-ranging patrols to try to provide advance warning against incursions by the law.

They ate steaks done to order—a hard trick on the uneven heat of a campfire—and potatoes wrapped in aluminum foil and baked in hot coals. Afterward they sat smoking, taking their turns on watch, and wondering if they would be alive to see Christmas.

Birdwell wasn't ready for a patrol. He'd been awake till three in the morning playing poker and drinking, mostly drinking, with Rafferty. They'd sneaked into the supplies shed about an hour after lights-out, stuck burlap bags under the door to hold in the glow from their kerosene lamp, and Birdwell had produced his fifth of Jack Daniel's. He didn't like having to share one of his precious few hidden bottles with Rafferty—that skinny, loudmouthed, redhaired braggart—but it depressed him to drink alone. Once, the sentry had come by, and that dip Rafferty kept talking, and talking, till Birdwell had to smack him one to shut him up. And he still wasn't sure the sentry hadn't heard them. He might have heard and decided to wait till the next day to tell the Blue Man about it, not wanting to wake up the boss. In which case someone would be coming around to summon him anytime now.

And the sentry wouldn't have to *look* to see who was making the ruckus in the shed. He could look to see who was missing. And anyway, everyone would know it was Birdwell and Rafferty. They'd got in trouble more than once before.

The Blue Man'll never dump me, Birdwell thought. He knows I'm the best munitions man in the States.

He was standing shakily outside the barracks, had fallen in with the others, but not at attention, waiting for the patrol captain's inspection.

Birdwell had been a collegiate wrestler, years before; now he was approaching fifty, and his wrestler's build was sagging, his spare tire overhanging his belt, his sad blue eyes hooded with perpetual weariness. He wore the camp's special gray fatigues and black pullover cap. He stood shifting from one foot to the other, his hands crammed in his pockets, yawning, wincing as the sun threw spears between the treetops as it climbed with aching slowness into the sky. Rafferty, Marquam, Sloane, and La Cienaga stood beside him; Rafferty was glaring at him. He was pissed because of the smack across the chops and because Birdwell had skinned him out of two weeks' pay at cards.

Ostensibly, Birdwell was sergeant, an instructor for the Blue Man—Colonel Thatcher—and in charge of this mini-platoon. But the four other men had taken to ignoring his orders when there wasn't another superior around.

He knew it was because he was a drunk.

But what they didn't understand was: it wasn't his fault he was a drunk. It wasn't his fault he'd gone to seed, either. Most of it had happened in the last six months. It was like he'd aged ten years' worth in six months.

It was Tora's fault.

Birdwell shuddered, seeing her step out of the lodge, across the parade ground, down near the river.

The camp was set up to resemble a conventional military outpost as much as possible. There were six regulars' barracks and one big one for the trainees. The barracks were arranged in a U-shape with the big barracks at the bottom of the U and the lodge between the U's upper arms.

There was even a flagpole, but there was never a flag on it—and maybe that had something to do with the Blue Man's sense of humor. A notoriously twisted sense of humor. Everyone knew that despite his brisk efficiency, the Blue Man, Colonel Thatcher, was a little mad. Some said he'd gone mad on the day he'd been captured by a tribe of African rebels during the uprising against colonial rule in British Magresca. They'd tortured him, and then they'd tattooed his face with the indelible image of a blue skull. Hence his nickname.

Birdwell understood Thatcher's policy of running the camp as strictly military-discipline as possible. The trainees were from a variety of nations, and some of them were hostile to one another. They weren't allowed to talk among themselves much, except within assignment cells—each cell from a specific client—and they were kept segregated as much as possible, according to faction. But should one faction become aware of the presence of a rival faction, only military order would prevent bloodshed.

Not that Thatcher was squeamish about bloodshed. Oh, no. But he was squeamish about losing money. And clients were annoyed when the men they sent to be trained came back in a box.

Birdwell watched Tora walk through the morning mists toward the river. She liked to wander by the riverbank at dawn.

Tora, Thatcher's daughter, was half East Indian. She was twenty-five, but not much bigger than a thirteen-year-old girl; she was lithe and tiny-footed and almond-eyed and golden-skinned, with small, pointed, perfect breasts and a waist Birdwell could almost encircle with his two hands; her waist-length black hair swung behind her in a braid clasped by copper circlets. She wore her priestess's robes when she walked by the river; but she looked like a priestess no matter what she wore, even in her miniature army uniform. Now, with the mists curling around her ankles, her gait cat-smooth, she seemed more than ever a supernatural creature, and Birdwell remembered that once—once, just once—he'd held her in his arms, and he'd kidded himself into thinking it meant something to her . . . and the next morning she'd told him, yawning, she'd simply been curious about "what it was like to have an old man in bed."

That afternoon the Blue Man had granted three days' leave, and Birdwell had gone off the wagon.

"Birdwell!"

Birdwell winced; the shout hurt his hangover-throbbing head. He looked to see who was shouting at him. Morgan, the black patrol captain. "Come on," Morgan said, spitting. "Colonel wants to see you."

Birdwell swallowed and took a long, deep breath. He suppressed the urge to belt Rafferty again, because the skinny little fucker was laughing at him.

He shrugged and trudged off after Morgan toward the lodge, wondering why they hadn't called Rafferty over too. Maybe it wasn't the drinking; maybe it was Tora. Had Thatcher finally found out Birdwell had once slept with his daughter? But it had been months ago, and he wasn't the only one. Hell, half the camp . . .

The warmth in the lodge felt good in Birdwell's joints. He tried to pull himself together to look brisk and competent. He succeeded in looking nervous.

Thatcher was a tall, aristocratic Britisher, a man marked by bitter years of overseas service for her majesty. He had been drummed out of the Royal Corps of Halberdiers—the stories varied as to why.

He was waiting in the lodge's common room. The Nine were there with him, seated at the long table.

Thatcher stood at the head of the table, his back to a crackling fire in a wide stone fireplace. The flames leaped yellow and blue to either side and behind him; it looked, for a moment, as if he were standing among them. The skull tattoo showed with frightening clarity, blue as a corpse. The effect was increased by his saturnine face, his up-angled eyebrows, his black eyes, his cold, toothy smile. He wore a tight-fitting gray military uniform of his own design and knee-high black riding boots. He stood with his hands on the back of a chair that was pushed up to the table, and his smile drained all the warmth out of the room. The Blue Man's smile called up despair in Birdwell.

"Birdwell," said Thatcher softly, as if talking to himself.

"Yes, sir?"

"One time too many, Birdwell," Thatcher said briskly.

"Sir?"

"I can still smell the booze on you. From here."

Birdwell said nothing.

"So you want to leave us, Birdwell?"

Birdwell blanched. "No, sir."

"You have a choice. Leave us or be tested."

Birdwell's gut lurched. *Tested*. He looked at the nine men sitting at the table. Nine impassive faces. Most of them would be bored behind that impassivity. A few would be enjoying this. There were two Arabs, a Scot, two Americans, an Armenian, two Sicilians, and an Englishman. All experts at terror; each one responsible for some atrocity—or several atrocities—laid to those who employed the Blue Man's services.

And it was these men who would decide what his test was to be.

Birdwell shivered. But the alternative . . .

"The test," he said. "I'll take the test."

4
The Test

They had left the Jeep behind in a rocky alcove at the foot of the cliff, camouflaged under brush cuttings and net. Now they were toiling up the spare wild-goat path zigzagging the face of the steep ridge. Each of them carried a heavy pack of weaponry and supplies. It was about ten A.M., and the sun was hot on the back of their necks. Snag, a sort of human almanac, insisted they would have fairly good weather for two weeks—and then all hell would break loose.

Sullivan was in the lead, Snag just behind him, then Merlin and the stolidly trudging Rolff. On a spur of rock just below the lip of the ridgetop, Sullivan paused and turned to survey the view. It was a strange landscape, broken up as if by some Japanese gardener, with patches of black lava flow reaching out in spreading veins from the ridge's base. They were on the lower slopes of Mount Chemwa; on the other side, with luck, they'd find the terrorist training ground. Miles to go yet.

The greenery below was shrouded with mist and pocked with patches of arid ground. The Rogue could be seen flashing like a comet's tail in narrow, twisting streaks of silver—one of the fastest rivers in the USA. The other three kept going up the thin, steep, gritty trail, passing Sullivan one by one, each giving him a side glance as they wondered what was on his mind.

Sullivan was thinking that the fool's skirmish with the hunter was a bad omen. There were a lot of strange, uncontrollable factors in this landscape. You could plot and plan every move of your campaign, and then find the whole thing broken down because of some freakish mischance. A misplaced bootstep—

There was a shout from above, and the sound of rocks thudding into dirt.

Sullivan turned and braced himself—two men were sliding down the hillside toward him, falling out of control. Merlin and Snag. Merlin had stepped on a bit of unstable rock, and it had given way under him. He'd fallen against Snag, and the two men were tumbling down the steep path, coming at Sullivan with enough force to sweep him off the spur of rock and over into space.

It was a good four-hundred-yard fall to the rocks below.

Sullivan drew his knife.

He jerked the big double-bladed knife from his belt sheath and stabbed down with it, at Snag—driving it between Snag's ankles and into the grit and dirt of the almost vertical trail. Putting all the power of his arms and chest into that overhand slash downward, he drove the knife into the ground to the hilt a split second before Merlin and Snag—shouting, clawing to regain their feet—came tumbling one atop the other into Sullivan.

Braced against the spur with his boots, anchored with the knife, Sullivan took the five hundred pounds of hurtling mass in his arms and shoulders, grunting, hanging on to the knife hilt for—literally—dear life. Their combined weight was increased by the heavy packs they carried. For a moment Sullivan

45

was sure it was too much. He felt the knife blade pulling free of the dirt, felt the tug of the earth's gravity at his back, visualized the three of them going in an absurd tangle of limbs over the edge, separating on the way down to fall into the ruthless rock fangs waiting below. . . .

And then Snag reached out and got a knob of granite outthrust from the rock face just above them; Merlin managed to plant the rubber soles of his boots against the spur Sullivan held on to—and the crisis had passed.

Rolff was already lowering a rope to them.

Ten minutes later they were over the lip of the ridgetop, sitting at the base of a weather-twisted Joshua tree, smoking and thinking. All of them thinking the same thing.

Thinking: So close. So many ways death can come.

Birdwell stood on the bank of the river and thought more or less the same thing: Lot of ways to die in there.

Here the Rogue was all white water, a blindingly fast rushing over and between boulders and the rocky bank; only twenty yards across in this stretch, in some places deceptively shallow. Deceptive, for the next step might take you in far over your head. The river rushed here with such force that a man falling into it would be swept out of sight around the bend in less than five seconds. It was a river that was notorious for the lives it took in the white-water competitions. But in those competitions no one tried to raft down *this* stretch.

There was a cable stretched over the river here, secured to pylons sunk into the bank at both sides. The two-inch metal-thread cable was stretched not quite taut a foot and a half over the surging waters.

There was a metal ring, three inches in diameter,

loose on the cable. As Thatcher and three men from the Nine watched, Rafferty attached the hook on the harness over his chest to that ring and slung a leg over the cable. He stepped off the bank and shinnied horizontally over the water, both legs and arms hooked over the cable, dangling just above the rushing waters. A few minutes more and he'd reached the boulder outcropping on the far side of the river, almost at the opposite shore. There, as per Thatcher's orders, he unhooked his harness and sat back on the boulder to wait. He didn't look happy about it. Not at all.

He was worried, for good reason. Because Birdwell's endurance test—a test to see if he "still had the grit that makes him worthy of membership in our staff" —was this: he had to cross the river on the cable to Rafferty; he was to take Rafferty on his back and bring him back across the cable, coming hand over hand, with no help from Rafferty. Both men would be partly immersed in the water. They would not be allowed to use the harness and ring. They would probably be swept to their death.

A man stood on the opposite shore, rifle in hand, to shoot either or both of the men if they tried to make a run for it in the brush on the opposite side.

Birdwell wore his fatigues. When they became wet, there'd be that much more weight to carry across.

"Well, Birdwell?" Thatcher said crisply.

Tora was watching from the sun-porch on the second floor of the lodge.

Birdwell glanced at her and knew he couldn't back down. He nodded and moved toward the cable.

The river seemed to increase its noise, like a hungry animal roaring when it sights its prey.

It boomed and shooshed and echoed these noises into a hundred variations; a spray was thrown up by its dashing, to make rainbows in the midday sun in its rising mist; the mist dewed the cable, making it slippery.

Birdwell took a firm hold of the cable a yard out from the pylon and slung himself onto it, hooking both legs over, hanging underneath like an opossum, working his way across the swaying line feetfirst.

The river frothed hungrily for him, just under his ear, pausing now and then to lap at him with a tongue of water splash.

The trip across went fairly quickly. Ten minutes of aching palms and swaying on the cable, and then he stood beside Rafferty.

Rafferty looked at him, and his lips moved angrily. The booming of the river blotted out the words, but Birdwell thought he was saying, "It ain't fair. You got me into this!"

Birdwell snorted and shook his head. He stretched once, then went to the cable and looped an arm over it. He stood at the edge of the boulder in a cloud of spray mist. He could smell the river smells, the wet organic life in it; the rest of the world was soundless, all sound curtained by the white noise of the Rogue River.

Birdwell looked over his shoulder at the bank and saw the man with the gun. Merguela, an Argentinian. Dark face with a white grin in it, a bit of grass stuck in his teeth, the rifle cradled in his arms.

Just looking for an excuse to use that rifle.

Birdwell caught Rafferty's eye and made an impatient gesture with his chin: Come on! Rafferty glanced at the man with the gun, then at the men across the river. Then he threw his arms around Birdwell's neck and jumped onto his back, locking his feet around his waist.

Birdwell took the cable in the pit of each elbow

48

and crossed his arms overtop it, locked each hand on the opposite wrist. Then he slung himself into the water.

It was like stepping into the path of a speeding freight train.

He shouted, but it was lost in the roar of the hurtling white water around him. The battering water pressure fought to jerk him free of the line, and nearly wrenched his arms from their sockets. He was half-strangled by Rafferty's grip about his neck. He forced himself to move, to struggle for a grip on the slippery rocks under his feet. Already his legs were going numb, and he was being swept out behind the cable, his legs lifted almost horizontal, like laundry on a drying-line in a high wind. He bicycled his legs forward, against the current, and found purchase on a slippery upthrust of rock under his toes. He inched along the line, his arms screaming with pain, the cable burning through his clothes, rasping, the water jerking cruelly at him, Rafferty a hateful burden on his back, the roar in his ears. . . . He wanted to let go, to give it up, to allow the river to sweep him to his death against the jagged rocks behind him—but then, through the mists boiling up from the white water, he saw *her* face on the other side. "Prove that you're worthy," her eyes seemed to say.

He kept on. Inch by inch, through icy hell, the river's white fire, moving toward her large seductive eyes.

Those brown eyes seemed a million miles away, and it took a million years to reach them.

He slogged on through pain, his heart working against all reason past the point where it should have burst, the weight on his back like a great railroad spike between his shoulder blades, the creeping numbness threatening to stop his limbs from working forever—and then he was within reach of the pylon.

He had made it!

But Rafferty, panicking, pushed off from his shoulders toward the pylon, flailing for it.

The kick against his ribs as Rafferty pushed for the safety of the pylons threw Birdwell off balance. His legs were wrenched from their slippery purchase and snapped out behind him. The suddenness of it tore him loose, and then he was in the water, upside down, windmilling, lost in a kaleidoscope of bone-chilling white, free of Rafferty and the cable but caught up now in the merciless grip of the Rogue River. He felt it pry his lips apart and force water into his lungs. Darkness closed in on him, and he was ready to surrender—until a cannonball impact in his belly smacked him up above the waterline and forced the water from his windpipes. He had struck a rock, by chance hitting it with his fat-padded belly. The water behind rammed him against the rock, vising him onto it, holding him in place, keeping his head just above the flashing white waterline. He waited till the river would give up toying with him, tire of its cat-and-mouse game, wrench him loose to smash him into death in the narrows ahead.

A noose lowered to dangle above the water not far over his head. For a moment he thought he had hallucinated it—the River God was telling him it was about to strangle him. And then he knew that someone was lowering a lifeline to him from a tree branch overhanging the water. He had just enough strength to slip his left arm through the noose. He felt it tighten and begin to lift him free. The water sucked at him, jerking his left arm from the shoulder socket. The pain hit him with a wall of night, and he blacked out.

The sign said: "DANGER! TURN BACK! VOLCANICALLY UNSTABLE AREA!"

Sullivan stared at it for a moment, then bent to look at it front and back, closely. There was no serial number on it. And yet it was printed. Anything printed by the government should have a serial number on it. Nothing. So probably the Blue Man had placed this here to frighten away intruders.

The signs were nailed to trees and lightning blasted snags along the back of the ridge. The trees had thinned here—the ground was rocky, with the occasional thicket of scrub brush. Goat paths and erosion trails wended between the brush and the outcroppings.

There was no obvious proof of the sign's claim so far, but the twilight seemed thicker than it should have at this elevation—probably with smoke residue in the air. And the air was faintly tainted with the rotten-egg smell of sulfur springs.

Sullivan, Rolff, Merlin, and Snag moved up the hillside; just on the other side they would find fumaroles and hot springs. And, Sullivan suspected, lookout patrols for the Blue Man.

Snag led the way now. He carried a heavy pack, and he'd been drinking for weeks before the mission. But he pushed on with brute determination, insisting on showing he could carry his own weight. Sullivan could see it was painful for him—he was out of condition. But he said nothing. Sullivan sensed a monumental pride in the Indian.

The shadows deepened as the four mercenaries crossed the ridge and began to descend the other side. Here Sullivan could see streamers of blue and yellow smoke trailing in the westerly wind from rocky pocks farther down the slope, and on the flanks of Mount Chemwa, looming over them.

Snag led them into the deeper shadows and kept the boulders and copses of trees between them and the valley below.

The valley, between the arms of the ridges, bottomed out a half-mile below them; it was thick with pine and Joshua stands. Away to the northwest there was a feather-white flash from the Rogue River, just a piece here, an edge there, glimpsed through the clumps of greenery. They could see nothing of the training camp, but it would be on low ground, well hidden by trees, and partly camouflaged.

When the purple shadows began to close into a pool of darkness around them, Sullivan called a halt beside a bubbling hot springs on a terrace of rocky earth halfway down the slope. "Here," he said. "This way we don't risk a fire. The springs'll keep us warm. . . . But don't throw down too close to the crater, the moisture might corrode your weapons."

The crater itself was about twenty feet across, mottled on the interior, below the seething waters, with intricate encrustrations of lime and calcium deposits.

Despite the warmth from the hot springs, which bellied against the slope over them, a sharp wind knifed in during the night, so that the men standing watches huddled into their jackets and cursed when the wind maliciously snuffed their cigarettes.

At seven the next morning Sullivan spotted a black ribbon of smoke against the horizon, rising from somewhere between the trees and the far riverbank. It was a long way from the hot springs, and it was thicker, darker smoke—Sullivan judged it to be from a furnace or a big fireplace. Too large a fire to be a small camp.

"That's them," Sullivan muttered, scanning the area with his high-powered binoculars. He glimpsed a spear of silver that might be an antenna—or possibly a flagpole.

A flagpole?

Sullivan shrugged, and left the boulder to return to the camp. Snag and the others had just packed up their gear. "We're splitting up," Sullivan said. "Snag and I head down into the trees. You two head northeast along the ridge. Avoid clashes unless you're spotted. Make sure they're not hunters, if you decide to go after them. Ideally, observe but don't let yourself be observed. We'll meet back here at thirteen hundred hours."

An hour later Snag and Sullivan, having cached most of their gear near the campsite, were moving quietly through the underbrush at the bottom of the ridge. Sullivan pulled up short, frowning.

He heard a strangely out-of-place sound. A grown man, sobbing.

The sound came from the other side of a screen of yucca and scrub pine growing along the edge of a steaming hot spring. Someone camped near the rim of the spring, Sullivan guessed.

He signaled Snag, carrying the M16, to move around to the left; Sullivan, carrying the AK47 automatic assault rifle, set on manual single-shot, turned to the right—as an afterthought he hissed after Snag: "Just cover me, don't interfere unless it looks like I'm going down."

Snag nodded, and crouching, slipped between the serrated bayonet-shaped leaves and was gone from sight.

Sullivan moved low, in the cover of the yuccas; the plants were widely spaced enough to permit easy passage. He came to the edge of a small clearing and peered out through the leaves. A man in fatigues, with a gray crew cut, a sagging gut, and an alcoholic's bulbous broken-veined nose, was squatting beside the seething spring staring into it. He had given up crying; now he simply looked desolate. He sat on his haunches. In his left hand was a half-empty fifth of Jack Daniel's. An M16 lay on the rocky ground just out of reach. A sling hung uselessly from his left shoulder; he was evidently supposed to have that arm bound up.

Sullivan made a mistake then. He thought: The guy's broken up inside. He's limp. Harmless.

Sullivan stepped from the screen of bushes and stood within arm's reach of the stranger, the AK47 lowered. "We have to talk," Sullivan said. "I need to know—"

That's as far as he got. Birdwell came roaring around at him, teeth bared, eyes red, fury in him grateful to find a release.

He kicked out and knocked the rifle from Sullivan's grasp, then swung the whiskey bottle like a nightstick, overhand at Sullivan's head, amber liquid gurgling down his wrist.

In that moment Sullivan could see he'd misjudged the man. He was drunk and going to fat, but he was *big*, and he had years of conditioning for combat. Sullivan could see that in his bent-legged stance and the attack claw he made with his left hand. All this flashed through Sullivan's mind in a split second as he stepped under the down-swinging arm, caught it in a judo hold at the wrist, and levered it over his left shoulder. The bottle fell away into the spring. The big man went over, but landed on his feet and twisted out of Sullivan's attempt at a half-nelson. "I'll show the bastards!" he was shouting. "I'll show 'em I can still cut it!" He spun and shot a karate jab at Sullivan's throat. Sullivan had the edge in speed. He sidestepped and stabbed two stiffened fingers at the small indentation in the base of Birdwell's throat. Birdwell gagged and swayed, flailing blindly at Sullivan. Sullivan guessed that the man's left arm was recovering from some injury—there was the sling, and the arm moved more stiffly than the other. He chopped at the shoulder, not hard enough to break anything. But hard enough. Birdwell gasped and clutched at the arm, staggered backward. For a moment he tottered on the edge of the hot spring. Sullivan wanted the man alive for questioning—he stepped in and grabbed his right wrist, jerked him away from the boiling water. And was rewarded by a knee to the groin. Birdwell laughed rustily as Sullivan bent reflexively over the explosion of ice-shard pain in his crotch. He kicked at Sullivan's head.

Despite his pain and temporary partial paralysis, Sullivan ducked the blow, then charged under Birdwell's upraised leg, driving his lowered right shoulder into the sole of his opponent's boot—at that angle Birdwell's leg was locked for a moment, and he was off balance. The gambit sent him piling over backward, arms windmilling, his upper torso going into the boiling mineral waters. He shrieked and jerked up in a fast sit-up, wrenching out of the cooker.

He rolled onto his side, groaning, turning red from the waist up. He wasn't badly burned—he'd been in only long enough for a first-degree.

Snag stepped into the clearing, grinning. "Nice to know you're not invincible, Sullivan," he said.

Sullivan was still bent, recovering from the blow to his groin. He straightened, wincing, and said, "Uh ... cover this asshole. He's treacherous." He bent for his AK47. "You got a first-aid kit, Snag?"

"Sure thing." Snag took the kit from his belt, and keeping his M16 trained on Birdwell, moved to pass the metal box to Sullivan.

Birdwell was sitting up, glowering at them. He

looked dizzy but didn't seem to be in shock. Sullivan dropped the kit at his feet, pointed the AK47 at him. "Take off that shirt and put some burn dressing on."

"Fuck off," Birdwell growled.

Sullivan raised the AK47 and fired, making chips of rock jump between Birdwell's outstretched legs.

Birdwell didn't so much as twitch. He kept on glaring.

Sullivan was impressed. But he pretended not to be. "Okay. So you're a tough guy. But listen: I got a feeling you're pissed off at somebody. Something tells me it just might be the same people I'm pissed off at. Maybe we could work together. I could use another man. I can pay. And you're good."

Birdwell was mollified. He reached for the first-aid kit. "Maybe," he said. "Just maybe. We'll talk."

The light shot of morphine Sullivan gave Birdwell cooled the pain of his burn and had the side effect of making him dreamy and talkative.

They had come back to the camp. It was early evening. Snag was on watch; Rolff and Merlin sat on low humps of rock to Sullivan's right and left. Birdwell sat across from them, wrapped in a sleeping bag, propped up against a boulder. The hot springs bubbled between them.

Rolff and Merlin had reported seeing three men on a patrol or some kind of military exercise at the edge of the pine woods to the northeast. The men had been wearing gray military fatigues and black knit caps. All three men had carried rifles and grenades; Rolff and Merlin hadn't been seen by them.

"He kicked me out after they had to fish me from the river," Birdwell was saying. "Because he said it was proof I couldn't cut it at the base anymore."

Birdwell closed his eyes and spoke as if talking in his sleep. "Said I failed the test. But it was Rafferty's fault, jumping prematurely like that. They all knew it was Rafferty's fault. That bastard Thatcher just wanted to put me through hell, that's all. Wanted to humiliate me. And then he kicked me out of the camp—and he didn't kill me." He opened his eyes and stared with horror into the vapors rising to one side. "He didn't kill me!" He shook his head. "The bastard. The rotten bastard."

Rolff arched his blond eyebrows quizzically; his normally impassive face showed a rare moment of amazement. "You *want* him to kill you? Why? Because you failed?"

Birdwell glared at him. "Failed? I didn't fail! He should've killed me to show he had respect for me! To show he was scared of what I might do, or who I might talk to on the outside! But it was like . . . like he figured I was such a coward, so afraid of him, I wouldn't say nothing. And he expects me to take this recruiter bullshit seriously. 'You can still be useful to us alive, Birdwell,' he said. He wants me to find new instructors and go out to scare up more business. A wimp's job. A goddamn recruiter. A salesman." He shook his head. "Thatcher can fuck himself. No way I'm gonna do that shit. I'm just thinkin'. I was supposed to head out of the territory, rendezvous with one of his operatives in Seattle. But fuck that—I'm just gonna sit here till I think of something. Something to fuck him up good."

"You never thought of going to the feds?" Merlin asked, lighting a cigarette.

"You kidding? That'd be the pussy way. I want Thatcher's blood myself."

Sullivan nodded. "We can take you where you want to go. But you'll have to play a game with Thatcher for a while. *Pretend* you're recruiting—and then you recruit me. You'll give it a couple days, then report back to him that you just ran into the perfect potential instructor in a bar in Portland. Me."

Merlin looked at Sullivan with surprise. "But Thatcher'll know who you are. If he sent out some men to off you . . ."

Birdwell frowned. "Maybe not. I'm not sure about that assignment. But there was an Irish guy they gave it to—a guy named Spike. I heard he got himself offed. Nobody knows by who. Thatcher doesn't concern himself with the details of every kill. One of the Nine would've overseen that. But chances are he'd know who you are only from a photo. That Spike guy, way I remember, was the only one who actually got to the target area. Now, that photo'd be pretty old. And if you was to change your looks a little, come in under a different name—my recommendation ought to get you in." He grinned. "Yeah, from inside you could bust 'em wide open."

"But why was it," Merlin asked, "that they set out to kill Sullivan in the first place?"

Sullivan locked his eyes on Birdwell.

Birdwell shrugged. "Not sure. Except it was someone outside who paid the Blue Man—I heard that much. It works like this: there's the Nine—that's nine guys in charge of training and also for what the Blue Man calls international operations. Or interop. Mostly they do interop. Usually they're spread out around the world, but just now all nine are in the camp for special training session. Now, interop means that people pay 'em to do a terrorist hit. They do the hit, real professional-like, and some organization, the one that paid 'em, takes the credit for it. That way the politicians that paid the Blue Man to send the Nine out for an interop, they don't

58

risk their asses. And the guys who do the hit—maybe blow up an embassy or machine-gun a newspaperman—they couldn't care less about the political statement, see. They're just pretend terrorists. Terrorists for hire—they'll do it for anybody. Funny thing is, sometimes you'll get somebody who'll pay the Blue Man to stage an interop for the opposition. Like the right wing pays the Blue Man to plant a bomb and then calls in a claim for the left wing—in order to, you know, discredit the left wing. And the left do it to the right." He laughed, then yawned.

Sullivan shook his head in disgust.

Merlin said, "And the camp trains terrorists for sincere causes too, right?"

"Sure," Birdwell says. "All kindsa crazies."

Sullivan stared grimly into the setting sun, shimmering amber-golden along the ragged back of the ridge above them.

How many lives had been lost because of some fat oil sheikh's political caprices? How many had died because some half-assed nation's amateurish "intelligence" service had hired the Blue Man to pull its dirty tricks for it, indifferent to the suffering of the people caught in the middle? Some family off to market in a Middle Eastern bazaar, walking by a car which blows up, taking half the people in the bazaar with it. Just so many more statistics. . . .

The bastards. As if there weren't enough crazies in the world—without starting a Rent-a-Crazy! And how many genuine terrorists had been primed for their mission of horror in this quiet, primeval setting? It had to come to an end. For Lily. And for all the other innocents butchered as Lily had been.

The darkness closed in on them, cold as Sullivan's determination, falling over the training camp below them.

* * *

The next morning dawned clear and cold; steam from the hot springs was absorbed into the endless blue of the sky. They had just finished coffee when Merlin, lying on his belly atop a boulder, scanning the valley with binoculars, hissed, "Sullivan! That patrol's on the southwestern fringe of the woods—paralleling it. Moving this way. Three hundred yards off."

"Pack it up," Sullivan ordered. "Move out."

Birdwell winced from time to time, his skin still sensitive from the burn, but he moved about the camp doing his part, and seemed to have accepted Sullivan's command. They had his word that he'd cooperate—but was his word enough? Sullivan had sized him up, and suspected he might be treacherous. He just might betray them to ingratiate himself with the Blue Man. Or to that woman he'd told them about. He'd sounded as if he were in love with this woman Tora. A man in love is irrational, unpredictable. He'd bear watching.

"Hey . . ." Merlin hissed. "They just grew by four. Total of seven now. Still coming this way."

"We oughta take the assholes," Birdwell said, his voice acid with hatred.

Sullivan shook his head. "Not yet. I don't want to tip our hand till they're vulnerable. Make sure nothing's left behind here. The camp clear? Not a single cigarette butt. Okay . . . this way."

Shouldering his pack, assault rifle in his hands, Sullivan led them down the hillside, threading through brush, keeping low, always maintaining a screen of boulders and foliage between them and the enemy below.

It was only too probable, Sullivan reasoned, that his men had been spotted. Anyway, he couldn't take a chance on it. He had to assume the patrol had been sent to check them out. The number of men in the patrol had increased, possibly indicating that some platoon commander for the terrorists had decided to increase the strength of the investigating team should the strangers prove to be dangerous. So far, the terrorists probably thought the strangers were a bunch of drunk hunters out for elk.

Sullivan hoped they liked surprises.

A boulder-strewn ravine bordered the pine woods, a sort of dry moat between the woods and the hillside. The patrol was moving along the lip of the ravine in the shadow of the wood; the wood was roughly diamond-shaped and came to an angle of the diamond just a few hundred yards ahead of the terrorists. The stand of trees where the woods cornered would provide good cover, if Sullivan could get his men onto the other side from the enemy without being seen. He veered off to the north, his left, and moved into a trot. The others trotted along close behind him, dodging quickly, one at a time, across the occasional open spaces.

They worked their way down the slope, and Sullivan raised a hand to signal a halt behind a cluster of hut-shaped boulders on the edge of the ravine, just across from the woods.

Sullivan sidled between the boulders and bellied down on a bed of gravel and windblown pine twigs to peer cautiously out of a stone crevice. Across the ravine, six men wearing gray fatigues and black knit caps were hunkered down between two pines just inside the woods. He could make them out only in patches—an arm here, a rifle there, their helmets; the rest was locked in by shadows. But he counted six helmets. Where was the seventh? Reconnaissance? Sullivan frowned. That could be a problem. He had to stop all seven of them, to head off advance warning to the camp. Ideally, the Blue Man shouldn't know anyone was gunning for him until he felt the bullet breaking his skull.

Birdwell had told him that the patrols went out for two to three weeks at a time, and maintained radio silence except in emergency. They didn't want to tip off the feds, should anyone be monitoring their radio band. So Sullivan could snuff this crew without alerting the Blue Man that anything was wrong for up to three weeks. And by then, if Sullivan's plan worked, the Blue Man would be a corpse, his nickname becoming a physical reality. If. Yeah, if. The best-laid plans of mice and men . . .

A seventh man came into sight a hundred yards south of his partners and jogged up to the terrorists' temporary camp. He spoke to a man who was probably their commander, and pointed into the woods.

Sullivan frowned. Did they think the intruders were in the woods? But moments later the seven men were filing out of the trees and between boulders to enter the ravine.

Sullivan nodded to himself. That was better. It'd be easy to cut them down when they were at the bottom of the ravine. He could catch them in a crossfire.

Sullivan wriggled out of the crevice and returned to his team. The men gathered around him and listened intently as he issued orders, speaking in low, clipped tones. "Birdwell, you know those woods better than I do, so you take the rear-strike team. Take Snag and Merlin . . ." Sullivan hesitated, looking at Snag. "But then, a guide isn't signing on for—"

"Hey," Snag broke in, "I'm with you . . . all the way. I trust you, man. You got my gun too."

Sullivan nodded. "Okay. Birdwell, Snag, and Merlin head down into the ravine, double-time. Those guys are going it slow. Get across fast. Cut through the woods, come out in back of them, and they should be on the far side of the ravine, almost to the top where it meets the hillside, with their backs to you. When we open fire, that's your signal. Shoot to kill. Take off your packs before you go. Pick 'em up later."

"Better get the radioman first," Birdwell told Sullivan. "He'll be the third or fourth man."

Sullivan said, "I'll take care of that. They're just going down into the ravine now—and it's around a corner from you. I don't think they'll see you. Go: double-time!"

The three men slipped off their packs, grabbed their automatic weapons, and ran in single file between the high boulders edging the ravine. Sullivan led Rolff, who was silent with grim anticipation, back the way they'd come for fifty yards, then cut back to intersect with the terrorists about where they would emerge from the ravine.

Sullivan was carrying out his plan almost absent-mindedly. He was already thinking ahead, to the infiltration. He was sure the ambush would come off without a hitch. He had forgotten one of his own mottoes: Never be too sure.

5
Double Ambush

They were in chill blue shadow, and the morning was still cool, but Snag was sweating.

He wanted a drink. He had that kind of thirst—an alcoholic's thirst. You could drink a gallon of cold water and still be thirsty. Birdwell had the same problem—you only had to look at him to know. But the guy seemed fully prepared for the action. His eyes were bright, and there was a nasty smile on his lips as he toiled through the woods beside Snag. He took the lead as they broke from the stand of trees, keeping low so the humps of boulders at the edge of the ravine would hide them should their targets choose to check out the rear.

This is it, Snag thought. Can I cut it?

He had been confident of himself up till now. But with the return of the thirst, that confidence had melted away.

He took a deep breath, narrowed his eyes, and checked his weapon. He was as ready as he'd ever be. This was his chance—his chance to prove he was more than "just another drunk Indian." He sensed that Birdwell had something to prove, too. Birdwell's left arm was still screwed up—some medic at the camp had put it back in its socket, but it was still swollen—and he'd have to do most of his shooting with his right. Maybe this Sullivan hadn't made such a wise decision, putting Birdwell in charge.

Wondering about that made Snag a little less certain about Sullivan's authenticity. When you were with the guy, you didn't question him. He had a presence of authority, of knowing, that made you put aside any misgivings about anything he was saying. But what if these men *weren't* international terrorists? What if it were some paramilitary group—maybe bona fide survivalists? If that were the case, Snag would be participating in murder.

But they were carrying M16s—no survivalist group could legally carry automatic weapons. And now, as he crouched beside Birdwell and Merlin behind a screen of brush, watching the men work their way up the steep face of the ravine's far side, he could see that these men were an organized military team, and something about them signaled: predator.

They were after someone—and when they found him, they'd kill him.

And yet . . .

His doubts were shot away as gunfire erupted from the lip of the ravine opposite and a little above them. Sullivan and Rolff had opened up on the enemy.

Merlin and Birdwell were lying belly-down on either side of Snag; Birdwell had wedged the M16 between two rocks to give him the support his injured arm couldn't give, and Merlin was firing a sniper's rifle, squeezing off one shot at a time. Snag pushed aside his doubts, got into the one-knee-down firing position, sighted the M16—and lowered it. There was nothing to shoot at. It was all over. The seven men were scattered at various heights down the farther face of the ravine, draped bloodily over boulders or sprawled arms akimbo on heaps of rubbled rock.

One of them tried to lift himself up—Merlin

squeezed off another shot, which echoed like mad laughter up the ravine and split the man's spine.

There was no other movement from the seven men in gray fatigues.

Snag was staring down at his gun, thinking: I didn't get off a shot. He got to his feet, and heard someone behind him shout, "Over there! Snipers!"

A bullet spanged off a rock face beside his head, and a commanding voice said, "Freeze! The next one is gonna blow you away!"

Snag turned slowly around.

There were five men in gray fatigues, each one with a rifle snugged to his shoulder, the sights on Birdwell, Merlin, and Snag.

Snag dropped his rifle.

Rolff shook his head glumly. "I saw at least five of them, Sullivan. The other team's been taken prisoner. Looks like the backup came in from the woods behind."

Sullivan swore softly. "That's my fault. My goddamn fault. That seventh man who came out of the woods—he must have gone to get a backup team. But from what Birdwell said, there shouldn't be more than fifteen men in any given area. . . . Did you see a radio?"

"No. But that doesn't mean there isn't one. Like to have a look?" He offered the binoculars.

"No. We go in to eyeball it. Fast."

"You think maybe the gunshots will alert the camp?"

"Doubt it. From what Birdwell says, they do a lot of target shooting when they're out on training patrols. Come on."

They ran back to the place where Birdwell had led his team across, and crossed in his tracks. By the time they reached the woods, both men were

66

slick with sweat and breathing hard. They paused in the shadows under the trees to rest and reorient. Sullivan signaled for silence. They listened.

The woods were quiet—something had frightened the animals into silence. Then Sullivan heard a rhythmic crackling sound, and the faintest murmur of male voices. Couldn't be more than twenty yards off.

Sullivan whispered, "You hear 'em?"

Rolff nodded. "How do we hit them?"

"Stick close to me. When I signal you, we flank them. If the lay of the land is good."

"Okay." Rolff took a long swing from his canteen, passed it to Sullivan, who took only a small mouthful.

Sullivan checked his weapons. He decided on a Uzi machine pistol and a .45. "Use your machine pistol," Sullivan said, "but don't rake—we don't wanna drill our own. We've got to hit them hard and from close up, almost eye to eye, to get it done quick. Otherwise they might get Merlin and the others up for shields."

"Suppose they're not tight on the trail? I might—"

Sullivan shook his head. "If they notice one's missing, it might tip the ambush. And we've got to ambush them. They're more than twice us. Come on."

The woods here consisted mostly of elegantly thin pines and a pungent blue-twigged bush with searching thorny branches. But both Sullivan and Rolff were expert at moving through dense underbrush. They stashed their rifles, and armed with pistols, machine guns—the pistol-sized kind—and knives, they penetrated more deeply into the woods, moving as noiselessly as possible toward the faint sounds of the enemy's passage.

A ground mist was rising as the morning sun

rose, and it thickened about them as they went, moving down a gentle slope into an unreal landscape of tree trunks straight and silvery as bayonets, ghostly fog, and the shadow of impending bloodletting.

Snag thought, over and over: I failed. I blew it. I didn't fire a shot—and I got myself captured.

They were being marched down the middle of a tree-lined gully, waist-deep in fog, Merlin and Birdwell single file ahead of him. Three of the gray-uniformed soldiers were behind him, two in front of Merlin. They carried M16's and .45 pistols. The prisoners had had their hands tied behind them with canvas straps.

Snag stole a glance over his shoulder at the man behind him; he was swarthy, hook-nosed, dark-eyed, thin. Middle Eastern, Arab or Persian. This was the one who'd kicked Snag four times after he'd tied his wrists. The patrol commander had said, "Cut it out. You bust him up too badly, we might have to carry him. The Blue Man'll want to interrogate them."

The Blue Man. The legendary international terrorist—Snag had heard about him from a friend who was in the Army's antiterrorist strike team. "We figure he's in Libya, or maybe Kuwait," Snag's friend had said. It never occurred to them the guy might be in the States.

So now Snag knew. Sullivan had been right.

Snag staggered when the killer behind kicked him in the small of the back.

"Face front!" the man snarled. Snag turned and staggered on.

A knot of pain jumped in his back with every step. You'll pay, you bastard, he swore silently.

But deep down he thought it was more likely the bastard would be torturing and then executing him, kicking his body into a shallow grave, maybe before tomorrow's sunrise.

Sullivan gave Rolff a curt hand signal; Rolff faded to the right and into the brush, moving with the grain of the branchings, keeping low . . . and unreeling a ball of twine behind him. The communication cord.

Sullivan was hunkered down behind a fallen log on the low rise above the gully. He could see the first of the terrorists about forty yards below and to the right, wading through ground fog, his gray fatigues making him look like a part of it, rifle in his hands; he was watching the brush, and seemed nervous, craning his head this way and that way, probably realizing he'd made a mistake leading his party into the gully. That nervous watchfulness might make it hard to pull off an ambush. Unless Sullivan could make it work against them. . . .

Ambush. Ambush is a science, and Sullivan had once helped write a field manual about it. *The ambush should be sprung when as many of the enemy as possible are in the killing ground and the range has been reduced to a minimum. There must be no halfheartedness or premature action.*

They were twenty yards away now, moving more rapidly. The patrol leader was clearly looking for an opening in the brush to either side, hoping to take his men out of the ambush-pregnant gully.

If he did that, he might slip past to a more defensible position. They could hold Merlin and the others hostage. Terrorist reinforcements would come . . .

Troops must select a comfortable position and remain in it—sometimes for hours—without smoking, moving, or undue noise. Troops must be trained to ignore flies, ants, et cetera, remaining unmoving without lapsing into sleepiness. Alert immobility . . .

Sullivan hunkered motionless. He would have

liked a cigarette and he would have liked to scratch. He made no move. He blinked; that was all.

Now the dark-skinned patrol leader was almost abreast of Sullivan—he looked to be South American, and the other patrol members seemed a diverse selection of hard cases of several nationalities. The leader was about ten feet lower and twenty feet to the right of Sullivan.

Sullivan breathed slowly, taking long breaths. His Uzi was cocked, held not too tightly in his hands.

The man in the lead was probably one of the Montoneros terrorist group from Argentina; the second looked Irish—IRA. Was it really probable that representatives from normally unrelated terrorist groups could work together? But Sullivan remembered a CIA brief Malta had shown him a few years ago—Malta had started out working for the CIA—something like: "A loose alliance of international terrorists who seem to cooperate in use of personnel, funds, arms, intelligence, and operations, despite their having widely varied ultimate goals . . . they are linked via the Carlos group."

But now they'd moved into position, and it was no longer time for thinking about them. That was the difference between Jack Sullivan and other enemies of terrorists—Jack Sullivan didn't simply wonder about them. He did something about them. He acted.

The first thing he did was to reach down and pull a piece of string.

The string ran twenty yards through the brush. Rolff had laid it down carefully so it wouldn't snag; Sullivan tugged it hard.

It was as if he'd pulled out the pin on the human grenade that was Rolff.

Rolff opened up with his machine pistol at a range of less than a yard; he'd slipped down into the gully

70

itself, moved in on his belly, hidden by fog and ground brush and ferns. Now he popped up like a jack-in-the-box, machine pistol yammering in his right hand, in his left the old WWII German P-38 he always carried, spitting a shot here, another there, between short bursts of the automatic. Two terrorists jerked in circles, spun by 9mm slugs in opposite directions, faucets of blood opening up on them in a red gush.

Sullivan waited, counting to five, fairly certain the lead terrorists would either turn to face Rolff or plunge in panic through the gully—it went both ways. The leader turned to face Rolff, and so did the Irishman; a third, running past the prisoners, jerked Snag to his feet—all three of the prisoners had thrown themselves flat when the shooting started—and dragged him off down the gully, a hostage.

The Montoneros and the Irishman were firing toward Rolff from the partial cover of a tree that had fallen from the rise to angle into the gully. Rolff had taken cover behind a red-dirt hump of the gully wall. M16 slugs kicked fantails of red dust and gravel into the air.

Sullivan was moving in closer, the bursts of gunfire covering the sound of his approach. He'd lost sight of the fifth terrorist and Snag. The man had dragged Snag into the woods.

The Irishman turned, checking behind him, just in time to be thrown back against his partner by a Uzi burst at close range, a spiked fist ripping into his belly. Both men went down, and Sullivan didn't bother to sort them out. He raked back and forth till the huddle of men was silent, unmoving, almost unrecognizable.

Sullivan turned away, shouting at Rolff. "Did you see where—?"

He was interrupted by a rattle of gunfire. He

glimpsed muzzle flashes off to the left as he threw himself down. Bullets shredded the moss and made a salad of the fern leaves to his right. He humped forward, worming through the moss to the wall of dirt marking the edge of the gully, then got to his feet and, heart pounding, zigzagged to the left and up the slope, into the woods. Bullets slammed into the tree trunk beside his face, stinging his cheeks with splinters. He threw himself down, rolled, came up set to fire . . .

And froze. Snag was between him and the enemy.

He could see the yellow-haired, white-browed German, his face sunburned and now shiny with sweat, over Snag's shoulder. A Baader-Meinhof gangster, probably, from West Germany. He was leveling an M16 at Sullivan's middle.

But then Snag threw himself backward, pile-driving his right shoulder into the pit of the terrorist's gut. The M16 was knocked aside, its burst ripping into the trees overhead.

The two men went down, but Snag was up first, kicking. The rifle spun away into the ferns. Snag's hands were still tied behind his back. "I'll take care of him, man," Sullivan said. "Move aside."

"The hell you will," Snag snarled. "This asshole pissed me off." He stood over the prostrate man, who was trying to back away on his elbows, and then raised his right foot, jabbed it down again hard, crunching into the terrorist's Adam's apple with his boot heel. The man gurgled and clawed at his throat. Snag stomped down again and again, as if squashing a particularly energetic cockroach.

Finally, when the terrorist's throat was a flattened mash of gore and bone splinters, he was satisfied, and turned moodily away.

Sullivan cut him loose. "Uh . . . yeah. I guess you *were* a little pissed off," he murmured.

72

Snag sighed. "I'm sorry I let 'em get the jump on me."

"It was my fault. I figured it wrong. But we got 'em all. This bunch didn't have a radio, did it?"

"Didn't see 'em use one."

"Then we can get the jump on the Blue Man."

6
The New Man and the Blue Man

"Gentlemen! Good to see you are all intact!" said Malta in his courtly way as he opened the door. The five men filed into the motel cabin and arranged themselves about the room in varying postures of weariness, sitting on the bed, the chairs, leaving Malta standing. Malta and Birdwell looked at each other. Both of them raised their eyebrows.

Sullivan introduced them and roughed out Birdwell's involvement in the new plan. The mercenaries were once more in civvies, drinking beer, and thinking about supper when the knock came on the door.

Sullivan lifted a corner of a windowshade and peeked out. There was a stout county sheriff on his porch, glaring impatiently at the door.

Sullivan swore and muttered, "Watch what you say. It's the law."

Sullivan answered the door. "Well! You a game warden? We didn't shoot a goddamn thing up there, and the fish were—"

"I'm not the game warden," said the sheriff. "I'm the cops. The county sheriff. My name's Hartz." He extended his beefy hand to be shaken, though there was no friendliness in his sagging red face. He had piecrust ears and gray hair marked with the band of his hat, which was in his left hand. "Mind if I join your little party?"

"Not at all," said Sullivan, hoping he was convincing. "Maybe you can give us some advice how to change our luck on the local fish."

Sullivan stood aside and let the sheriff ease himself through the door. His gun belt jangled its cuffs as he moved.

Sullivan waved a hand toward the seat he'd vacated.

The sheriff sat and accepted a beer. But the expression on his face never altered. He might have been going into the witness box for the prosecution.

He looked at Snag. "You here, Snag?"

"Doing a little guide work," Snag replied easily. "Didn't do a very good job." He grinned.

Hartz nodded. "Some local fellas died a few days back. And some others were pretty badly busted up. Bones broken, light concussion. Dave Moran and a fella from the lumber camp name of Dud Hauser." He looked at Sullivan.

Sullivan shrugged. "Don't know 'em," he said.

"Oh, you met 'em," Snag said, chuckling. "The guys who picked a fight at the bar."

"That who that was?" Sullivan said. "We knocked 'em down, but we didn't kill 'em. There was a whole bar watching. It—"

"I know," Hartz broke in. "Self-defense. They didn't die at the bar. Their van ran off the road up in the hills—or this Hauser's van. Hauser and Moran got free. The others couldn't get out in time, burned up with the van. Now, Dave the . . . Dave Moran says that it was an accident, some gas can caught fire. But the word is, he and this lumberjack set out with Arn and Lon to find you boys after that fight. They were armed, I hear. And that Moran, he's a bad liar. I think he's covering something up. Maybe he wants whoever ran that van off the cliff for himself—after he gets out of the hospital. He said something like that to a nurse . . ."

He broke off to swig his beer, but never took his eyes off Sullivan. Fishy blue eyes that gave Sullivan a chill.

Snag shook his head. "You say that was right after the fight in the bar that van ran off the cliff?"

"Not long after."

"Then they're in the clear. They were with me, right here, getting drunk till about five in the morning. Played some cards, planned the fishing trip, drank some whiskey."

"You swear to that in court?"

"Sure."

The sheriff stared at him. "I've known you a long time, Snag. Never knew you to lie. Well, we'll see." He set his beer mug aside with a clack, and grunting, got to his feet. He went to the door, opened it, then paused, turning back to say, "The whole bunch of you stick around till we get this cleared up."

Sullivan frowned. "How long'll that take? We wanna hit those trout streams again."

"A few days to see if the ruling of accidental death holds. I suppose it just might hold." He looked at Snag. "They were assholes anyway."

He left, and Sullivan stared after him, thinking that maybe Sheriff Hartz was all right after all.

Then he turned to Snag and silently shook his hand.

Five days later, the judge was satisfied that the deaths of the two rednecks had been an accident. Snag told Sullivan the news only minutes before Birdwell, his arm free of the sling, arrived with news of his own.

It was a Saturday morning, sunny and brisk. Sullivan, Merlin, and Rolff were sitting around the kitchen table in Rolff's cabin cleaning their guns.

Snag opened the door for Birdwell, who didn't bother with greetings. "They're ready for you, Sullivan," he said as he stepped into the room.

"When?" Sullivan asked pensively.

"Anytime. They were surprised I found somebody so soon—I told them I ran into an old Nam buddy at the airport in Portland. Made up a story. Told 'em you had a dishonorable, that you did time in San Quentin, that you'd worked for the Mob but didn't like it much, that you were looking for merc work and you didn't care who you worked for."

"How'd you get in touch with them?" Snag asked.

"Special radio frequency—they monitor it at certain hours, once a week. Codes."

Sullivan nodded and said nothing more till the weapons were cleaned and stowed away. Then he brought out the map of the wilderness area around the camp. "Let's go over the routine again. Three assault plans and three contingency plans. Now, Plan Alpha has a number code for initiation . . ."

Birdwell's route to the camp took him and Sullivan along a faint trail paralleling the course of the Rogue River. The trail was tortuous. Snag, Merlin, and Rolff had penetrated the attack zone by a different route and would wait outside the perimeter for Sullivan's radio signal.

Sullivan wondered more than once if he were walking into a trap. Birdwell might have set him up in order to get back into the Blue Man's favor. But that didn't fit with what Sullivan had observed about the man. He didn't want the Blue Man's favor. He wanted his death.

Sullivan shrugged. The risk of betrayal was only one of a dozen risks he was running on this mission. He'd never been involved in anything more dangerous.

And now he was marching into a stronghold of international terrorism, completely unarmed.

It was late afternoon on the second day of the hike in. Birdwell had declared they'd hit the camp by sundown.

Now and then Sullivan glimpsed the river through the evergreens, rumbling and hissing and forever shattering itself on rocks. The trail turned left and they got nearer and nearer, till the sound of the river was almost a roar—it was an explosive sound, but there was the shoosh of waters moving in it too, and suddenly, in his imagination, Sullivan was back in the Mediterranean, swimming toward the cabin cruiser, eager to tell Lily about the dolphins he'd seen, eager to hold her in his arms, and then . . .

And then she didn't exist anymore. One moment she was waving at him, eager for him to come back from his swim, and the next she was blown to atoms, as if she'd never been at all. . . .

It had been a long swim, a long road, a long trail from that murder to its avenging. To this barbed-wire fence and the four men in gray fatigues manning its checkpoint.

Strands of antipersonnel wire stretched across an aluminum frame about eight feet high; the dark-skinned soldiers were carrying Skorpion machine pistols. Their C.O. motioned, and two of the men unlocked the gate and slid it aside. Birdwell followed Sullivan into the perimeter. The gate banged shut behind them, and Sullivan knew there was no turning back.

"We searched him twice, sir. He's clean," said the gate C.O.

The Blue Man nodded and leaned back in his chair. He looked closely at Sullivan. Sullivan had grown a short beard, and he kept his right eye squinted, as though it were a nervous tic. His face had been badly scarred in the last two years, since Lily's death. But the Blue Man said, "You look familiar."

Sullivan shrugged. "FBI files. You got access?"

"Actually, I do. Maybe that's where I saw you. I'll have to ask my source there if he has a file on"—he glanced at Sullivan's false I.D.—"on Richard Stark."

They were in the den of the main lodge. Thatcher, the Blue Man, was sitting behind his desk, his hands palm down on the desktop, his face, in the flickering light from the fireplace, looking inhuman with the blue skull tattooed on it.

Sullivan stood before the desk, looking as nervous as he was expected to look. Two men armed with Skorpions stood behind him.

"Birdwell says you're good."

Sullivan nodded.

"Birdwell's a good judge of men. Bad judgment with bottles. But we don't know if we can trust you. We need loyal men here."

"I'm loyal to anybody I work for. That's what being a merc is all about."

"You have experience training men?"

Sullivan nodded. "In Special Forces."

"What's the story behind this dishonorable discharge of yours?" the Blue Man asked, watching him carefully.

Sullivan—Richard Stark, to Thatcher—stiffened and shook his head. "I don't see what that's—"

"Everything. We need to know everything about you. Who you fuck, how you do it, and what bath soap you use afterward."

Sullivan pretended to hesitate. Then he snorted in derision. "Story I tried to sell some bitch from a VC prison camp to a slaver. Lot of crap."

"I see. Tell me this. Birdwell says you're an armaments expert, that you know them all. How do you operate a World War Two–vintage Panzerfaust?"

"The old German rocket launchers? It's essentially a thirty-two-inch tube with a five-inch bulb at one end. You line the target up with the rear sight against the pin on the warhead. You arm it by cranking back the lever up top, jam it forward to fire. The ammunition—"

"Enough. The armaments sergeant will give you a few other basic tests—assembly and disassembly, that sort of thing, probably no problem for you."

"When do I start work?"

"After you pass the special tests. We only hire special men, Stark. Only the best, the toughest, the hardest. The special tests establish that you're one of them. The salary here makes it worthwhile, I assure you. If you wash out . . ." He paused long enough to take a cigarette from an ornate box, lighting it with a gold lighter. ". . . you die."

Sullivan turned to look at the two men with Skorpions behind him. "These guys took that test?"

"No. They were not applying to be part of the command unit here."

Sullivan said, "Okay. Whenever you're ready."

"The first test," the Blue Man said, blowing a gush of blue smoke toward the ceiling, "commences right now. Fritz . . ."

One of the guards said, "Yes, sir," and shoved Sullivan toward the door.

He was driven outside and shoved against a bullet-pocked brick wall across from the lodge, part of a fallen-in storage building. The guard cradling the Skorpion submachine gun took a firm grip on it and raised it to firing position.

Colonel Thatcher had come out into the dim light of the compound between the barracks. The coal of his cigarette glowed red in the darkness of the doorway as he watched.

Sullivan waited.

"After I give the command to fire, cut him to pieces," Thatcher said.

"Yes, sir," said the guard.

"*Fire!*"

7

And on Your Report Card, D Stands for Death

Sullivan knew what to do.

Nothing.

He didn't even allow himself to blink as the bullets gouged the wall to the right of his head, stitching holes up the brick, over his head, down the other side, nearly blasting his right ear off—the gunman tracing Sullivan's outline in gunfire. The bullets dug into the brick and mortar, shrapneling it to pepper Sullivan's neck.

He didn't move.

The sound was deafening. The gunman was squeezing off bursts that cut into the brick between Sullivan's right arm and waist—a space of three inches.

Sullivan held his breath.

The gunman's clip emptied; the echoes of the automatic fire died away. Sullivan shrugged. The Blue Man smiled. The first test, the test of his nerve, was over. The worst was yet to come.

"Give him some dinner," Thatcher said, "and rotate a guard on him. I'll supervise his test at dawn."

"Father? Who is he?" A woman's voice.

Sullivan looked around, trying to place the source of it. He could hear her, but he couldn't see her. The only light came from a bulb mounted on the cornice of the lodge; there was a small porch light glowing on each of the barracks across the compound.

And there was a half-moon. Not enough to hold the night back. The woman's voice, silky and soft and catlike, was coming from the deeper pit of shadow on the second-floor terrace of the lodge; he could just make out a slender female shape against a muted glow of candlelight. Candlelight? Why was she using candlelight? The camp had electric power generated by a water wheel in the furiously pushing river. She was just a voice in the shadows, and the candlelight seemed appropriate for the sort of voice she had. As his eyes adjusted, Sullivan could just make out the swell of her hips, a moonlight-tinged curve of one of her breasts. She was naked, though it wasn't a warm night, clothed only in darkness.

Sullivan felt her eyes on him.

He wondered if she knew he had a hard-on.

"Who is he?" she repeated.

Sullivan very nearly blurted, in the strange mood that had come over him: *I'm Jack Sullivan.*

But he kept silent as Thatcher said, "His name's Stark. He will be testing for instructor status tomorrow."

"Wake me at dawn, Father. I want to see."

"Good night, my dear."

Jesus Christ, what a family! Sullivan thought.

"C'mon, man," said the guard, friendlier now. "Let's get some chow. . . . Sorry I had to push you. Part of the scenario."

Birdwell and Sullivan ate silently, under guard, in the kitchen of the mess hall. "Gets real complicated, making up the food in here, all these na-shun-alities," the guard remarked. "Keepin' 'em from slittin' each other's throats gets complicated too . . . but except for a few rival PLO factions, we don't get much outright hostility, long as they don't start talkin'. If they start talkin' between groups, they get what the Blue Man calls your i-dee-oh-logical conflict, if you follow me. They oughta shut up and learn their trade, that's what I think. . . . How's that stew?"

"It's all right. What's the test tomorrow?"

"Don't know. The Blue Man usually makes it up—doesn't do it the same twice."

After that they went to an empty cabin, with just two bunks, and tried to sleep. Birdwell was to leave in the morning, and Sullivan would be alone, surrounded by his enemies, without an ally on the inside.

He gave up on trying to sleep, and that's when sleep came, bringing with it dreams of a dark-skinned, petite girl with a submachine-gun strap over her shoulder where another girl would have the strap of her purse.

At dawn Sullivan was awakened by a bayonet.

The cold steel blade jabbed him twice in the ribs, not hard enough to break the skin. He sat up and looked back and forth between the two men wearing black ski masks, bayoneted M16's in their hands.

Sullivan was not impressed.

He assessed the M16's with a professional eye. They were showing signs of rust, and the stocks were splintery and scratched. Sixties vintage, he guessed, left over from the Vietnam war. A great deal of the arsenal of international terrorism consisted of weapons abandoned by American troops in the hasty pull-out at the end of the Vietnam war, collected by the Vietnamese, appropriated by the Soviets, and sold to Soviet puppets and sympathizers.

"Your guns need better care than that," Sullivan said, standing.

"Shut up," said one of the terrorists, jabbing a gun butt at Sullivan's belly. It was like a college hazing; they were trying to frighten him.

Sullivan flexed the muscles of his stomach and absorbed the impact of the rifle butt, then jerked it from the guard's hands, reversed it, and slammed him across the side of the head with it. He could have killed him if he'd chosen to; he'd chosen to knock the man to the floor, where he sprawled, groaning, as the other snarled and raised his gun to fire. Sullivan knocked the barrel aside with the rifle butt and threw his weight behind a crossbar thrust, holding the rifle by the barrel and the stock, slamming his startled opponent across the side of the neck. The man fell, sputtering. Sullivan snatched the rifle from him, calmly stepped over him, and went out the door into the gray dawn light.

On his way out, he noticed that Birdwell's bunk was empty. Had he left the camp already? Once more Sullivan wondered if the man had betrayed him.

Thatcher, his daughter, Tora—Birdwell had mentioned her name only once, with notable bitterness— and a tall black man with a sardonic expression were waiting just outside. The black was Sergeant Morgan, carrying a Skorpion. "These are junk," Sullivan said. "They haven't been maintained properly." He tossed the rifles to the dirt.

The two terrorists came out of the cabin, staggering. Thatcher shook his head at them. "And he was asleep, too. Go back to the barracks, send La Cienaga and three others. Stay there till I call for you."

"But he—"

"Do as I tell you."

They went.

"Are you going to kill him for that, father?" Tora asked blandly. She was wearing a miniature gray uniform, completely changing its aspect. On her it looked like something appropriate for a disco. She wore sandals instead of combat boots. There was an

85

odd little smile on her half-Hindu face as she looked speculatively at Sullivan.

"Kill him? For walking over a couple of incompetents? No. But I considered shooting him for throwing those guns on the ground."

"They're junk," Sullivan repeated. "I can get you a good deal on some AK47's in great shape."

The four new guards arrived from the barracks, trotting, carrying Browning FN FAL automatic assault rifles, stubby little guns halfway between SMG's and M16's.

"Watch him, and don't let him get near you," Thatcher told them.

He turned and, his daughter at his side, walked off across the compound toward the river.

Morgan fell in beside Sullivan, the four soldiers just behind. Morgan chuckled and said softly, "You pleased him with that, I think. I would've thought he'd have shot you for it—for knocking those two clowns over. But you can't really predict the guy. A true English eccentric, our colonel. I got to warn you: he's gonna test you hard. Harder than usual. Harder than anyone else, maybe. Has something to do with your showing up so quick after Birdwell left. He's a little suspicious. And lately he's getting more and more paranoid."

They stopped at the edge of a woods of stunted pine, Joshua trees, and a few shattered yuccas. A thin sandy track led into the stand of trees. A few years back this section of the woods had burned, only a few hardy Joshua trees surviving. Most of what remained was first growth, and here and there the snags of charred trees standing like gloomy sentinels, black and ragged, over the others.

"In there, Mr. Stark, along this trail. If you are going to teach the setting of traps, you'll know how to avoid them, too."

Sullivan looked at the trail, then back at Thatcher. "I go in empty-handed?"

"Not at all!" He drew a bayonet from its sheath at his waist and passed it to Sullivan.

Sullivan hefted it. "Thanks a *lot*."

He turned to go into the woods, wishing he'd had coffee and breakfast—but in combat you had to be ready for action anytime. Even when you were hungry and sleepy. He paused and looked over his shoulder when Thatcher said, "Mr. Stark . . . don't kill any of my men you may encounter there, please."

"Are they going to play by that rule with *me*?"

"I fear not."

Sullivan snorted and turned away. He went cautiously down the path, looking at everything.

Looking to see if—

He dived to the left. The spike-clustered slicer whipped through the place where he'd stood a split second before. It swiveled in a lateral arc to dig itself into the soft trunk of a charred tree trunk so that ashes puffed in a black cloud over the trail.

How had he known it was there? He'd heard the soft *thwip* of the elastic trigger releasing. A familiar sound from Nam.

He got up warily, moved forward, hit a trip wire, and flung himself backward, rolling behind a tree as the "grenade necklace" went off across the trail—six hand grenades detonating at once, the air wild with singing shrapnel, fragments of metal slapping into the wood of the pine tree that sheltered him, pitching up dirt and a confetti of greenery.

"Son of a bitch," Sullivan muttered as the echoes of the last blast faded.

Then he took a deep breath and once more set off down the trail.

Twenty yards into the woods, and he detected no further traps. He was beginning to feel a little more relaxed, complacent—so he stopped stock-still, knowing that another trap must be close by.

He probed the ground ahead of him with the bayonet, and found the edge of a punji pit camouflaged with straw and pine needles. He started to go around it, and then stopped, thinking: They'd expect me to notice the pit and go around it.

A large, half-burned pine stood beside the punji pit. He found the wire noose nestled among the ferns at the base of the tree. He triggered it with the bayonet and watched it lash upward, jerked by the tensility in a bent tree limb, to snap against a spike in another tree trunk. It would have taken him by the ankle and slapped him against the spike.

Probing gingerly with the bayonet, looking for Claymores or more sophisticated land mines, he circled the punji pit and moved down the trail.

He was going down an easy slope now, the trail veering left toward the river, his feet skidding on the sand. He could see the white water leaping, a flash of white between the trees to his left. The ferns thickened, the greenery deepening near the river, and a ground mist began to curl up with the strengthening of sunlight. He no longer needed coffee or food; he was running on adrenaline now.

He came to a small stream, about two feet deep in the middle, which ran into the Rogue a hundred yards farther north. He had to cross the stream to continue the path . . . and he almost did. Then he cursed himself for a fool and backed up. He went belly-down on the trail, his nose within a few inches of the slow-moving stream's surface, and shaded his eyes against the light, looking into the water. He saw it.

A nylon line, barely visible in the shifting waterlight, cutting across the stream at the point most probable for fording. The line was a few inches underwater, tied to a stick at one end and to a fragmentation grenade, which was buried in the bank, at the other.

Sullivan had an idea.

Very carefully he searched the water with the tips of his fingers till he found the stick the line was tied to; even more carefully he bent the stick toward the grenade, making the line slack, and drew it from the muck, holding his breath the whole time. He let out a long breath when he'd gotten the line out.

He traced the line back to the grenade, then quickly dug the grenade out of the bank and planted it in a different spot a few feet down. He repacked the hole where the grenade had been, and stuck the trip-wire stick over it in plain sight, with half the nylon wire—which he cut loose with the bayonet—wrapped around it, as if a signal to the men he knew would be following him. A sign saying: I found your damned grenade trap. Very cute, but I'm not impressed!

Then he tied the remaining nylon to the firing pin of the relocated grenade and attached that wire to another stick hidden at another angle in the water. He finished up hurriedly, hearing muted voices from the trail behind him.

"Keep your voice down," someone hissed.

"He must've missed the trip wire and gone on, or by now he'd—"

"I said *shut up!*"

Sullivan slipped into the brush and hid behind a tree stump to watch. He was about thirty feet from the stream-trail intersection.

Four men armed with Skorpions—not the guards who'd escorted him from the cabin—came up the trail in single file. They paused at the stream. One of them swore and pointed at the stick in the bank with the nylon wrapped around it.

"He found it. Disarmed it."

"Good," said another man. "He's supposed to be passing a test, and he's doing it. You sound like you wish he'd got—"

"I'll tell you something, man," said the first one who'd spoken, "I think the Blue Man wants the guy dead. Nobody been tested so lethally before. I think he has a bad feeling about him. When he told me to set up the traps, I thought he—"

He stepped into the stream, to cross, and hit Sullivan's trip wire. Three feet in front of him, the stream bank opened up and threw itself at him, steel shards tearing through him and the man beside him, lifting both off their feet and tossing them with messy splashes on their backs in the water. The second two, unhurt, stared for a few seconds in shock at the dead men. The corpses bumped against each other like so much flotsam, the water clouding red around them.

"Shit, motherfucker!" one of the survivors burst out.

The other one said something equivalent in Arabic. They bent and, muttering, lifted the bodies out of the stream, set them on the bank.

Sullivan was pleased. If he worked things right, he could make it look as if the men had died running into their own booby traps—it had happened in Nam more than once. At least the Blue Man wouldn't be able to prove otherwise. And two more of the enemy were dead—two more terrorists, making a total so far of fourteen. How many more? Birdwell had said there were about fifty-five men in the camp. That left forty-one. Forty-one survivors of the organization that had killed his Lily—his Lily and hundreds of others.

But what about the girl—Tora? Would he have to kill her too? She didn't seem to be a captive. Birdwell

had said she was her father's accountant, invest-
ment counselor, and factotum. She was part of it.
But . . .

He put it from his mind. A problem for later.

The terrorists were debating what to do. "We go
on," said the Arab in a thick accent. "Blue Man
said we follow him, jump him if he gets to the trail
end. We do it."

Sullivan was already moving off down the hillside,
slipping silently through the brush, out of sight of
the men at the stream. After a while he found what
he was looking for.

Forty yards from the stream, two men crouched
behind a handmade camouflage screen constructed
of tree branches, ferns, and moss. Each man held a
green monofilament detonation wire which, Sullivan supposed, ran to Claymore land mines. Normally
such mines are detonated by a trip wire—but if
you're laying a trap for a particular man, a surer
way is to detonate the mines yourself by remote
triggering.

Sullivan frowned. Thatcher, it seemed, really did
want him to fail. Why didn't he execute him outright? "He's been getting more and more paranoid,"
Morgan had said. The guy was evidently going nuts.
Playing a game with him—a madman's game.

Sullivan had to move in before the two men at
the stream caught up. With luck, they were still
arguing.

He crept down the slope, easing past snags, anything that might make noise. Some sixth sense
seemed to warn one of the men, and he turned, just
as Sullivan was within reach.

He dropped the trip wire and reached for an
SMG . . .

Too late. Sullivan slammed the steel ring at the
grip of the bayonet between the man's eyes. His

eyes crossed and he slumped. At the same instant, Sullivan's left fist shot out, catching the other man on the point of the jaw with a precision learned in thousands of hours of martial-arts training.

He spun and fell inert.

Quickly Sullivan dragged the two bodies down the slope to the trail and laid them across it. He located the two Claymores—discus-shaped killing devices wedged on end at the base of trees so they faced one another across the trail. "The Blue Man wants to test my know-how with land mines," Sullivan murmured. "The M18A1 Claymore is an anti-personnel mine using one-point-five pounds of explosives to project seven hundred ten-point-five-grain steel balls over a sixty-degree arc for a distance of fifty meters at a height of one to two meters." He chuckled and settled down behind the screen.

The two terrorists who'd survived at the stream were coming down the trail. They spotted their fellows lying on the trail up ahead, and ran to check them out. One of the two stunned men was just then beginning to revive, sitting up and holding his damaged jaw. The Arab lifted the other fallen man to his knees, trying to revive him by slapping his cheek. The other survivor of the stream encounter was looking around. Then his eyes widened. He shouted a warning.

Sullivan jerked the trigger wires. The Claymores detonated.

A furious hailstorm of steel balls blew both ways across the trail, shredding the four men caught in it, making them jerk and dance and fall, shattered.

Sullivan jogged back to the stream, took each corpse there by an ankle, and dragged them down the hill to the second killing ground. He was sweating with the effort when he got there. Hopefully, it would look as if all six of the men had been killed by an accidental detonation of the Claymores. He hoped no one would look too closely at the bodies.

He rearranged the Claymore trip wires so it looked as if one had been set off by the victim. Then he headed off again down the trail.

When he came out on the other side of the wood, Thatcher, Tora, Morgan, and two of the guards who'd escorted him to the testing ground were waiting. They'd come by a roundabout trail.

Morgan and Thatcher looked at him in surprise. Tora looked at him with interest, the guards with respect.

The two other guards came out of the woods from behind Sullivan.

"Six men dead in there," said one of them. "Looks like they were blown up by Claymores."

Sullivan felt a chill when the Blue Man looked at him. The look said: "You did this."

Maybe it'll end here, Sullivan thought. It might be all over. One word from Thatcher, and the others will open up on me.

Sullivan said, "Looks like you need me bad here. If I'd trained those men, they'd never have set off those Claymores—not by accident."

"You killed them," Thatcher said, looking at him. The anger seemed to darken the blue-skull-face tattoo, so that it was Death himself accusing Sullivan.

Sullivan shook his head. "No. But believe what you want."

"Take him," Thatcher began, "and—"

"No," Tora said abruptly. "No, Father. I won't have you wasting any more valuable men. Men mean money. We need this one. If he killed those men, he only did what anyone would have tried to do. Because you set him up to die—"

"There was something all wrong about him . . ." Thatcher's voice was distant. There was an odd

93

distance, too, in his eyes. He seemed to be in a sort of trance.

"You haven't been well, Father," she said soothingly. "You got upset about nothing. He's one of us. I can feel it."

Thatcher turned away. "Very well, my dear . . ." He seemed to have lost interest. "I . . . I have to go back to the lodge." He walked hastily away, accompanied by Morgan.

The guards looked questioningly at Tora.

"Escort us back to the camp," she told them. "But hang back. I want to talk to him privately."

They nodded and backed off a few feet. Sullivan walked beside her back along the trail he'd arrived on. "I want to see the bodies," she said. "To see if you've done a thorough job."

Sullivan said nothing.

"There's one more test. A combination endurance and hand-to-hand-combat test. I'm sure you'll come through. I'll see to it the odds aren't stacked against you the way they were with this one. I think you'll be a big asset to us here."

She looked at him sideways.

"You've earned a reward," she said. She touched his arm.

"Good," he said. "Can I have it right away?"

She looked a little startled. "Well . . . now? This morning?"

"Sure. That's the best time for it. I'll have eggs, bacon, pancakes, potatoes, and coffee. Have them send it over to the barracks, okay?"

8

A Devil Among Us

"What's wrong with the Blue Man?" Sullivan asked softly.

"He's a junkie," Morgan said, "and I think he mixes cocaine in with it. It's makin' him worse and worse—more paranoid all the time. But don't quote me on that. Anyway, sometimes we don't see him for a week at a time, and Captain Bronnard gives the orders. Bronnard ain't bad—at least you know what he's going to do. This damn test is a waste of time. Anybody could see you're . . . Shit, here comes Bronnard."

It was noon. They were standing at the base of a steep hill. The hill was warted with boulders and steaming with boiling hot springs. A goat path ziggzagged up the slope through moraines of gravel and between boulders to the crown of the hill, at the foot of Mount Chemwa. It was hot, that autumn noon; there was a smell of sulfur in the air, which combined with the glare of sunlight off naked boulders to give the place a hellish aspect.

Bronnard was a gangly American without a nose—his nose had been shot away in some engagement somewhere. He kept himself pig-shaved and immaculately uniformed, and now he wore mirror sunglasses. He was coming down the hill with an Arab at his side. The Arab, a trainee, wore fatigues, looked like he'd have preferred a burnoose, and carried an AK47. He glared at Sullivan with un-adulterated hatred, and Sullivan guessed that the Arab he'd killed in that morning's test had been this one's friend—or lover.

Bronnard pointed at a backpack lying in the shadow of a boulder. "It's two miles to the top of that hill," he said, "if you follow that path. It zigs all over the damn hill. It's hot and it's steep. That pack weighs one hundred pounds. You got to get it up to the top—and there's gonna be some men try to stop you. Now, Birdwell says you're a top man on hand-to-hand. So if what he says is true, you should get through—these men aren't specialists that way."

But looking at the Arab, Sullivan suspected that the deck was once more stacked against him.

The guy had friends here, and the guy wanted to kill him.

Sullivan smiled grimly. "I'm ready for it," he said.

He went to the pack, and grunting slightly, slung it over his shoulders, closed the belt across his waist. This time he was not given a bayonet.

"Double-time it!" Bronnard shouted. "Go!"

Breathing deeply, Sullivan chugged up the hillside. He willed himself into the semitrance state that comes with regular rhythmic exercise; you become a machine, you recognize the pain of the heavy exertion only as a signal for the computer that runs the body, you ignore it and simply keep functioning, breathing regularly, fixing the eyes hypnotically on some goal ahead—a boulder, a bush, the shadow of a man . . .

The shadow of a man?

The man shadow stretched beyond a boulder's shadow where the path hooked back—someone hiding behind the boulder, twenty feet ahead.

Sullivan slowed, looking about the trail. He was just out of sight of the men waiting below.

He saw a glint of metal and stepped off the trail toward it. It was a thin metal fence rail, wrapped with broken, rusty barbed wire, two strands from some now-fragmented fence, each strand about ten inches long—perfect. He wrapped the wire more tightly, then pulled the post from the dry, loosely packed earth. It was about four feet high. He took hold of the lower end, just above the crust of dirt, and gave it an experimental swing. It went *whinnnss* in the air.

Sullivan considered laying down the pack. But he was supposed to keep it on for the full course, and someone might see him. Already the hundred-pound weight had coupled with his wearying muscles to feel like two hundred pounds. He hitched it up higher on his back, squared his shoulders, and went stalking the enemy.

He caught the man on the other side of the boulder by surprise, moving behind him off trail. The Arab turned when Sullivan's shadow fell over him. It was the Arab he'd seen below—the man had taken a shortcut directly up the hillside. He swung the AK47 up as Sullivan swung the improvised barbed-wire mace down at him. The man fired hastily, but the automatic weapon wasn't properly aimed, and the bullets hit the club instead of Sullivan's head. At a distance of four feet, the bullets struck the metal fencepost with tremendous force, sending painful shivers through Sullivan's fingers, knocking the shaft from his grasp.

Sullivan stumbled, and that stumble saved him. He fell past the muzzle of the AK47—the bullets sizzling by his ear. The Arab stepped back to get a bead on him, babbling in Arabic, and Sullivan used that moment to get his feet beneath him. He launched himself at his assailant, putting everything into it. He couldn't get up much momentum

97

with the heavy pack on his back, but the bulky weight of it plowed into the smaller man's gut, driving him back against the boulder. The Arab let out a gasp and dropped the AK47—it rattled down the hill. But the little Arab was tough, wiry; he wriggled away from Sullivan and got to his feet before the encumbered American could.

Sullivan was annoyed.

This little prick was costing him time and energy.

The annoyance became anger, the blood lust that made impossible feats possible for Jack Sullivan. The sort of strength that comes to a madman. Sullivan forgot the hundred-pound backpack. It was a soap bubble now. He leaped up, turned, bent, snatched up the barbed mace, and whipped it back around, catching the Arab—who was coming at him with a drawn knife—full in the face.

The barbs dug into the side of the man's face and ripped, pulling most of his face off. Bits of skull showed through the gory mask where his nose and lips had been. He screamed and flailed, the knife forgotten. Sullivan brought the mace back in a backhand swing, slashing its bristling killing end into the terrorist's throat, raking it out like overcooked chicken. Blood spurted, the man went wobbly in the knees and pitched over, rolling floppily down the hillside, his wounds coating with black volcanic dust.

Sullivan turned away. He was still mad. The world showed through a red haze.

Sullivan was fed up. First, he'd had to kill six men—literally before breakfast. He'd nearly been blown up several times. Now they were making him carry hundred-pound weights miles up a hillside while Arab assholes leaped out at him with AK47's. This whole undercover business didn't come naturally to him. It irritated the hell out of him. It just wasn't his style—but it was necessary. Necessary but infuriating. He had to take that fury out on someone.

He jogged up the trail, a killing machine, waiting for the next asshole to try something.

Three of them, coming at him from three separate directions, two from the right, one from the left of the trail, all armed with clubs.

Enraged, Sullivan swung the gore-dripping barbed mace at the nearest, a brawny Swede—the strands whipped at the man's eyes, blinding him with blood from a torn forehead. The man screamed and swung blindly. Sullivan ducked the club and at the same moment jabbed his mace like a spear at the gut of the man coming from the back. The man caught it full and bent over, momentarily trapping the mace in the folds of his stomach muscles. The third struck Sullivan hard across the shoulders, just above the backpack. Sullivan grunted, but didn't slow down. The pain only infuriated him more. He kicked out, caught the dark man with a vicious up-slice to the balls. The guy shrieked and fell back, clutching his crotch. But the Swede had cleared his eyes and slammed a club hard across Sullivan's left side. Sullivan caught the brunt of it on his left arm, which promptly went numb and hung like a slab of dead meat. Sullivan swore and jerked his mace loose from the gut of the one still gagging over it on his right—it ripped flesh, coming away, and the man howled with pain.

The Swede was raising the club for a whack at Sullivan's head. Sullivan leaped to the right—the Swede changed the angle of his down-slam at the last second-fraction, angling to follow Sullivan's movement, and impacting, as Sullivan had planned, with the head of the man whose stomach Sullivan

99

had slashed. Cracked sickeningly across the side of the head, the man went down like a brain-shot bull. The Swede blinked confusedly at his accidental handiwork, and Sullivan used the moment of confusion to step in and crack the metal club soundly across the bloody-faced blond's jaw. The terrorist jerked backward, spun, and fell in an untidy heap.

Sullivan turned to face the man he'd kicked—a dark-skinned man with large brown frightened eyes, who backed off, crossing himself, seeing the demonic rage on Sullivan's face, muttering, "There is a devil among us!" in Spanish.

The man turned and ran.

Sullivan shrugged, and still breathing hard—from anger, not exertion—trotted up the hill. "Come and get it, you sons of bitches," he muttered.

He knew he hadn't killed the two he'd left in the dust behind him. Both were simply out cold. Maybe he should go back and kill them. But he had to keep moving. Up, upward—he needed more enemy, more fight, active opponents. There was no satisfaction in braining unconscious men.

He was almost at the hilltop when he saw the man with the knife atop the boulder. Another Arab, probably a buddy of the first two. The man launched himself at Sullivan with a shriek and with an unbridled courage that surprised the American.

The Arab had made the mistake of letting Sullivan see him and underestimating the speed with which the big man could move, even saddled with a packhorse burden. Sullivan stepped briskly aside and swung the mace up to meet his assailant in midair, feeling for a second weirdly like a batter using a terrorist for a baseball. He missed the man's head, the mace swishing under and slugging nastily into the plunging Arab's middle. The Arab folded around it, tore it out of Sullivan's hand with the

100

momentum of his fall, and struck shoulder-first, gagging, wheezing for air.

Sullivan kicked him soundly in the side of the head—just hard enough to put him under for a while—then detached his mace from the shallow wound in the unconscious man's belly.

He got it loose just in time to face two more who ran at him shrieking, swinging clubs.

I'm gonna kill these bastards, Sullivan decided.

A rapid-fire spray of bullets kicked up dust eight times in half a second between Sullivan and the onrushing terrorists.

The terrorists pulled up short, skidding a little—both they and Sullivan turned to look at the source of the gunfire.

It was Bronnard, a smoking Skorpion in his hands. "That's enough," he said. "That's the end." He turned the gun toward Sullivan.

9

Fuck Me or Shoot Me, Make Up Your Mind

"Drop it or I'll nail you, Stark."

Sullivan dropped the mace.

"You weren't supposed to use anything like that," Bronnard said, nodding toward the bloodied mace.

Sullivan shrugged. "Was that first asshole down the hill supposed to use an AK47 on me?"

"No. You got a point." The grotesquely scarred terrorist nodded; the mirror sunglasses caught the sunlight, giving him eyes of fire. With a scabby skull-nose and suns for eyes he looked monstrous. "The hell with it. I'm stopping this bullshit now. You pass. Drop that pack and get the hell down the hill. You start work tomorrow morning."

"Stark?" A whispered voice in the darkness.

Sullivan sat up in his bed.

"Yeah?"

"C'mon outside."

Sullivan pulled on his fatigues and boots and stepped out into the night.

Morgan was out there, standing just outside the cone of light given off by the yellow bulb dangling from the wooden porch roof. Moths and mayflies dabbed at the light; crickets chanted a mantra. He could hear the rumble-rush of the river through the trees, like the sound of freeway traffic.

"What's up?" Sullivan asked warily. Was it yet another test?

In a way, it was.

"Tora," Morgan said. "She wants to see you."

Sullivan couldn't see Morgan very well, but he could tell, maybe by his voice, that he was grinning.

Sullivan said, "You got a cigarette?"

There was a rustling sound, and Morgan's night-colored hand came into the cone of light, passing Sullivan a cigarette. Morgan lit one for himself, his face illuminated from below in a match's flash. He extended the match to Sullivan, who puffed his own alive. Then Sullivan said, "Okay, let's go."

The two men walked side by side through the compound.

Sullivan was glad of the opportunity to study the camp's nocturnal sentry setup. He'd been lying in bed considering sneaking out to have a look around, maybe see if he could get over the fence to where he and Birdwell had cached the radio, send out a report to Malta and the others. But he'd decided he might be under covert surveillance here till they learned to trust him.

The time would come, as it came, despite all appeals, to most of the men on death row. The men in the camp were on death row—and didn't know it.

Now, looking casually around, he saw two guards stationed in front of the lodge, and two across the compound from one another, walking in opposite directions along the barbed-wire fence outside the U shape of buildings. There might well be others he couldn't see from here.

He suspected there were at least two guard-nests emplaced in the woods on the approaches to the camp, outside the fence.

"Suppose," Sullivan said, "her father finds out she brings one of the staff over after lights-out—"

"Don't worry about it. He knows all about it. He's so stoned out, he doesn't much care anymore. Truth is, she and Bronnard run the camp now." He sucked at his cigarette, making the tip pulse red, and added, "I think you ought to know—this girl got some strange ideas. She thinks she can 'know a man's soul' by making it with him. She slept with most of the staff in the camp, man. But listen: she never does it with any man twice. Not that I know of. So . . . I just thought I ought to warn you."

"Suppose I don't want to sleep with her. I don't like women who play games."

"I know whatcha mean. But . . . do it anyway. She pulls the strings on her old man. Don't make her feel rejected, you dig?"

Making his voice sound neutral, casual, Sullivan asked, "What does she do here that makes her so important?"

"She's taken over most of the business dealings. She got a talent for it. There's millions of bucks involved in this place."

"Yeah? Soviet millions?"

"Them . . . and others."

"So she's in charge of all the books, paperwork—they keep files?"

"Yeah. Somebody tries to open the lock on the files the wrong way, the whole thing incinerates. Man, if some of the clients knew about those files . . . Shit! They wouldn't like it."

They'd arrived at the lodge. A guard stood on the wide, railed wooden porch while another, strolling, circled the house. The guard nodded to Morgan, glanced at Sullivan, smirked, and went back to his yawning.

Sullivan was thinking: Files! She keeps files of

104

the cases! If I can get to those files, I can find out why they sent someone to kill me—someone who ended up killing Lily.

Morgan escorted Sullivan through the front door—which, like the rest of the building's exterior, was sided with cuts from unpolished logs—and into a plushness that contrasted with the building's log-cabin outside.

They walked over heavy tread-absorbing Persian rugs, past girandole mirrors, gold-framed, and heavily lacquered antique furniture, to a wide wooden stairway.

Sullivan felt a little awkward following Morgan up the stairs. Two hardened mercenaries, one taking the other to see a girl who looked delicate as a lotus flower. As if Morgan was a pimp for some Asian cathouse.

"A strange situation," Sullivan muttered.

"Yeah," Morgan said, nodding. They'd reached the top of the stairs.

He tapped on an antique wooden door.

"Yes?" Tora's voice.

"I brought him."

"Send him in."

Morgan said, "Go ahead." He didn't look at him.

Sullivan turned the brass knob—its face etched with a Hindu demon—and stepped into the room. He noticed that Morgan waited to see him go in. And Morgan had had to escort him right to the door. That meant that there was something else in the house they wanted to be sure he didn't see. The files?

Sullivan's first impression, stepping into Tora's room, was of soft blue light and incense. Jasmine incense.

The soft light was diffused by the silk curtains

105

dividing the room in half; the curtains were sheer, transparent. Through them he could see the blue lamp beside the bed and the outline of a window. She stood at the window, framed by the starry night sky, her back to him.

He heard her voice distantly; she didn't turn around to speak. "There's a door on your left. The bathroom. Go in there and make yourself ready. There is a robe."

Sullivan made the effort to check his temper. It annoyed him to have her tell him what to do this way, as if he were a servant. He didn't like to be commanded into lovemaking.

But he had to do it. And she *was* beautiful. . . .

In bed, anyway, he would do the commanding. He would do it without having to say a word.

He went to the bathroom, showered, toweled, and slipped into the robe hanging beside the door. He went into the other room, stepped through the slit in the azure curtains, and said, "You got a cigarette?" in a bored tone.

She looked faintly surprised. She had expected him to be devastated by her. She was lying back on a canopied double bed in the sheerest, clinging silk lingerie; the pearly lingerie was long, but slitted four places from the waist down, and he could see a golden expanse of thigh and the damp slit of her shaved pussy.

He didn't allow his eyes to linger on her; nor did he look embarrassed. He sat casually on the edge of the bed and said, "I need a drink."

"I've got something better." She nodded toward a hookah on an ornate brass stand beside the bed.

"Opium?" He shook his head.

"The liquor cabinet is at the foot of the bed." She sounded mildly annoyed.

He smiled and made himself a double Scotch on the rocks.

He returned to the bed, downed half the Scotch, clacked it down on the lamp table, and said, "You sure you're old enough?"

She stiffened and sat up. "Mr. Stark . . ."

He chuckled and said, "I just wanted you to sit up, so I could reach you more easily." He took her small shoulders in his two hands and drew her close. For a few moments she resisted, still irritated, unresponsive. But he drew back and looked her in the eyes. "Trust me," he said with perfect confidence.

He felt the sexual electricity in his hands. It was something you could project, just as you could project your *chi* force in martial arts—it was another wavelength of the same energy. He felt it pulsing strong in him, and she felt it too. Her resistance melted in the heat of his sexual glow, and she was suddenly soft under his hands. . . .

She was small, but she was limber, and there was strength in her as she writhed against him. She was compact and sticky-hot as she drew him onto her.

But he knew it was best to make her wait.

He chuckled, and drew back, and she said petulantly, "Where you going? Why do you laugh?"

He answered with another laugh, and lifted her clear of the bed, taking her under the arms, sweeping her up over his head. She was a petite woman, and Sullivan was bull-strong.

He lifted her up to the ends of his arms so that her crotch was just over his uplifted face, and he lapped at the insides of her thighs . . . at her labia and, with a marksman's precision, at her clitoris. She gasped—suspended eight feet in the air. She wriggled pleasurably in his big, rock-steady hands, immersed in the complete feminine surrender, totally in his control. Slowly, smoothly, he lowered her so that her labia left a stroke of dampness on his bearded cheeks, his neck, his chest, his lips sending pulses of sexual electricity into her, nibbling her small, perfect, uplifted breasts. Then he thrust his tongue hard between her lips, and she gave him hers. She rubbed herself against him like a cat grooving on a purr. He spread her legs with his hands, gently but firmly, and lowered her onto his iron maleness—both of them still upright beside the bed, she gasping, writhing, skewered.

She wrapped her legs around his waist, and he pressed her back against the bed, imprinting her deeply into the mattress. And for the first half-hour he went slowly, so slowly, grinding deep, and then faster, by degrees faster, deeper yet, and faster yet, until his hips went onto full auto, and ten minutes later he'd expended his clip, and it was time to reload. . . .

They lay limp, sodden, steaming, simply breathing. Sullivan was pleasured, and relaxed, but still he was thinking: Got to find out where the files are and how to get into them. But how, without making her suspicious?

There was one way. Make her exhausted, wait till she slept, and go out to find them. He sighed. It had been a long day.

She mistook his sigh, and touched his bristly cheek affectionately. "You are like no one else," she said. "I can read a man by the way he makes love. . . ."

Sullivan chewed a lip, worried that she had somehow "read" him, had realized that he was not who he seemed. Which would mean that he'd have to kill her, here and now.

"I can read men," she went on, "but not you.

108

You . . . overwhelmed me. It was like trying to say which way the wind blows when one is caught in a tornado."

"You trying to say you were blown away?" he asked, rolling onto her again. It had been a long day, and it was going to be a long night.

An hour later, just before dawn, her deep, regular breathing told him she was asleep. And in the muted light of the lamp beside the bed he could see her eyes moving beneath the lids in the unmistakable pattern of rapid eye movement. That meant she was dreaming.

He eased out of bed, holding his breath.

She stirred. He stood statue-still beside the bed, listening. Her breathing deepened, became regular once more. He slipped through the curtain, padded toward the door to the hall. He didn't bother to dress—he'd have to get back in bed with her soon.

He slipped out into the hall, wincing at the creak the door made, leaving it slightly ajar behind him. No one visible on the dark landing.

Was there a guard inside the house? He hadn't seen one.

He moved off down the hall. The first door he came to was unlocked. He opened it as quietly as possible and peered in. The faint light from the window showed an empty bedroom. He closed the door and went on. The next door was locked. That would be it, then. If he could find a hairpin, he could probably pick the lock. It was an old skeleton-key type. He started back to the bedroom, put his hand on the doorknob, and . . . *What was that noise behind him?*

Sullivan spun, snaking aside. The old British army saber flashed past his head, just missing his right ear, and sank its well-honed tip into the doorframe.

In the dim light filtering up from below, Sullivan saw a blue skull covered with beads of sweat, glaring at him with wild, sickness-maddened eyes.

Thatcher snarled and jerked the saber from the door, raising it high, pausing just long enough to whisper, "I'm going to cut off your head."

10
You Can't Kill a Bad Dream

Sullivan had less than a second to make up his mind.

Should he kill him? Sullivan was unarmed, and stark naked, but he knew he could disarm the Blue Man and kill him. The look in the Blue Man's face seemed to say that nothing less than killing would stop him. But if Sullivan killed him, it would blow the operation. It was too soon.

The saber came slashing down at him.

Sullivan ducked under Thatcher's arm, and was standing behind the Blue Man when the sword came down.

When you're unarmed, stark naked, and facing a maniac with a sharp saber, you move *fast*.

"He's gone!" Thatcher babbled. "Vanished. Another vision . . ."

He turned, and Sullivan jabbed him hard at the base of the head, with a stiffened thumb under the ear. Thatcher slumped, temporarily paralyzed by the nerve-deadening blow.

The saber clattered to the floor.

The front door opened below and a flashlight flared in the dark room.

At the same instant, the bedroom door opened and Tora stepped out onto the landing.

"What's going on up there?" called the guard, coming up the stairs.

"I heard someone chopping at the door," Sullivan told Tora. He felt odd, standing there nude with her father limp in his arms. "I came out to see what it was . . . and he hacked at me with his saber."

She nodded. She didn't seem surprised. "He hasn't been well. He sleepwalks. . . ."

Too much of some drug, Sullivan thought.

Thatcher groaned. "A jinni . . . I saw him . . . a nightmare . . . devil . . ."

"Another bad dream, Father."

"Kill him."

"You can't kill a bad dream, Father."

Sullivan picked Thatcher up in his arms and said, "Where to?"

"Down the hall, third on the left."

"Okay. How do I handle this tomorrow?"

"He won't remember anything tomorrow. Just put him in bed"—she yawned—"and come back to mine."

Sullivan nodded and carried the delirious man back to his bed, reflecting that if the Blue Man's customers knew the shape he was in, he'd soon go out of business—he was no longer reliable. If Sullivan chose, he could tell them and *put* the man out of business.

But that wasn't enough. Sullivan wanted him not just out of business—he wanted him out of the world.

He wanted him dead.

And yet he laid the Blue Man, one of the most important figures in international terrorism, down on his bed with the care of a nanny tucking in a sleeping child.

The time hadn't yet come, not quite yet.

"With a submachine gun, particularly a Thompson, which has a real kick to it, you aim low so that

112

when the gun jumps in your hand it will send the slugs higher than you aimed, carrying them into your target's torso," Sullivan was saying.

But to these men on the firing range he was not Jack Sullivan—he was Ritchie Stark, armaments and booby-traps instructor for the camp, a training ground for international terrorism.

It was a hot Indian-Summer afternoon, almost windless.

Sullivan stood with his six-man "trainee unit" a hundred yards outside the barbed-wire fence of the compound, facing man-shaped targets made of red cork painted to resemble policemen. He held a big, blocky tommy gun, a Thompson, vintage 1962.

This was Sullivan's third day as instructor. The first two days, Bronnard had watched over him, looking ugly and critical. Today Sullivan was on his own. There wasn't a trainee in the camp who would be leaving for thirty days. So if Sullivan's plans worked out, none of the terrorists he was instructing would be able to make use of the information he was giving them. Just in case, though, he was giving them only as much as he had to.

"This is a forty-five-caliber gun with an effective range of . . ." His voice trailed off as he saw Tora watching from the shadows of the pine trees beside the target range. She looked beautiful—wearing tight-fitting khaki shorts and a blouse tied up under her breasts, exposing her bare brown midriff. He couldn't read her expression. "Uh . . . effective range of fifty feet . . ." He was angry at himself for allowing the woman to distract him.

He turned the anger into firepower, demonstrating the Thompson on the cork targets fifty yards away, splitting them up the middle. Four bursts later, he broke off and said, "Most people won't be

113

so effective with an SMG at this range. It's not a weapon known for accuracy . . ."

But all the time, he was thinking about Tora. Morgan had said that she never had the same man twice. But Sullivan had been summoned twice more. She seemed both fascinated with him and, in some way, suspicious of him.

What really worried him was: it hurt to think he'd probably have to kill her. Despite his disgust at what she represented, at her knowing complicity in mass murder, he was becoming emotionally involved with her. And that could mean hesitation, indecision at a crucial moment.

Which could mean death for Jack Sullivan.

Merlin, humming to himself, tuned in the field radio to the special frequency he'd prearranged with Sullivan, and tried to sort through all the crackle and hiss. He glanced at his watch and muttered, "He's late. That's not good. He's always right on time."

Birdwell sat across from him, beside Snag and Rolff, in the dead grass within the rough circle of high, dusty, egg-shaped boulders atop the ridge overlooking the pine woods.

"I'm beginning to think the whole fucking scheme is crazy," Birdwell said. "By now they probably executed him—if he didn't get blown up. I heard rumors the night I was there . . ."

Rolff looked at him sharply. "What kind of rumors?"

Birdwell scratched his grain-sack belly and said, "Rumors about the Blue Man. And how he went over the edge. Drugs. All the time I was there, I never knew about the drugs—I shoulda guessed, the way he hounded everybody else. Me about my drinking, Garcia about his pot. People who're fightin' a drug problem are real goddamn self-righteous about everyone else's. I hear he lost that fight—it just got out of control. Started sending out for more and more. And now he's going off half-cocked all the time . . ."

"Dangerous for Sullivan—" Snag began.

"Seven-three-seven, this is John Bunyan," came a sharp voice abruptly. Sullivan.

"John Bunyan, this is seven-three-seven, reading on fourteen-oh." Merlin sang out.

"Seven-three-seven, we go with tertiary plan, but with variations. I'm sending out a little present to you, six or seven of them, and we'll give 'em a surprise party, with one or two deaths. Repeat, there will be no more than two deaths—there must be survivors. Same place as the last party at eighteen hundred hours tomorrow. Have you got the party costumes?"

"We've got 'em ready, John Bunyan. Tertiary plan confirmed, contingencies understood."

"John Bunyan out."

Merlin sighed and turned off the radio. "He's got freedom of movement now, anyway, seeing as he can get to that radio."

"What was all that about?" Birdwell demanded.

"We're going to dress up like your old friends. Gray fatigues. And we're going to make an ambush that isn't completely an ambush," Merlin replied.

"He's going to bring some men out to us?" Birdwell looked skeptical. "How? He's not authorized to—"

"I've got a feeling he's authorized for almost anything there," Merlin mused. "Didn't you say that Thatcher's daughter had a big influence in the place?"

"Yeah. . . . So?"

"They almost always fall for him, you know. Women, I mean."

Birdwell stared. Then he stood up, fists balled, and stalked away from the camp.

"What's bothering him?" Merlin wondered.

11
Maneuvers

"You said you were a believer in destiny," Sullivan said. "You believed in our destiny, together, here."

"I still believe in that," Tora said. They were lying in bed together, just after lights-out. It had gotten to be a routine. Sullivan no longer needed an escort. The other staff men glared at him covertly—all of them had been wounded by Tora. Tora was clinging to him, one slender brown arm thrown across his massive chest, her cheek soft against his pectoral, "I still believe we can make this place over again—we can do more than train them. We can control them, govern them. We can find a way to use them—to build a nation of our own somewhere."

Sullivan smiled. "Slow down, Madam President. We've got to get this business on its feet first. You say you're losing clients. We'll win them back by setting an example. We'll make this crop of trainees the best. They'll be the most dangerous men of their kind."

"But—"

"Look at me!" He took her by the shoulders and dragged her up to straddle him. He looked into her dark eyes, and for a moment felt lost in them. There were mysteries there. He knew, at bottom, she was just a fantasizing child. Hard as she was, it was only because no one was real to her, except her father. More than once she'd asked her father to kill someone who'd annoyed her. He'd done it for her. And she'd watched, distantly amused.

They were just toy men to her. The men she made love to, the men she'd had killed. Her father had taught her: Only we matter. Only you and I are real.

Now Sullivan was real to her too.

"Look at me!" Sullivan repeated. "Don't you believe I can do it? Do you doubt I'm strong enough?"

"Strong enough? I think you could tear the world in half with your bare hands. Strong enough, smart enough, skillful enough, my Ritchie. But it's not a question of confidence. It's a promise I made to my father—that no one under any circumstances, trusted or not, was to have access to the files."

"Your father is no longer sane. Promises made to him are no longer valid. Anyway, you want me to take over the camp. Right? I've got to do it my way. The way I know best. Which means I've got to have access to the files. I've got to understand each man's background—"

"Ritchie—"

"Do you believe in me?"

She sighed. "Yes. I'll give you the combination. For God's sake, be careful. If you don't do the combination correctly, the thing will blow up. It's valuable a hundred ways."

A hundred and one, Sullivan thought.

She looked troubled, so he sat up and shifted his hard-on so it skewered her from below, rewarding her confidence in him, telling himself: This is war. It must be done.

At nine the following morning, Bronnard stopped him at the gate.

There were six of them now, besides Sullivan.

118

Sullivan saw to it they were all Palestinians from the extremist PFLP, Popular Front for Liberation of Palestine. Ahmed, El-Mahud, Brihad, Soldad, Imman, Bruhol.

Bruhol, the rat-faced, yellow-toothed. Bruhol talked about ransoms, and nearly licked his lips, and it was obvious that he had none of the others' ideological fanaticism. He had been lured by the big money that sometimes flowed through terrorist hands. Young El-Mahud was a fanatic who asked detailed, intelligent, and chilling questions about the process of killing a sentry.

The others were like watered-down versions of El-Mahud or Bruhol. They waited, blinking in the morning sunlight, as Sullivan confronted Bronnard.

Bronnard's deformed, cold-steel, mirror-eyed face looked weirdly out of place in the fresh morning light. He stood at the gate in the barbed wire against a backdrop of green grass and blue-green pines, a living nightmare in paradise.

"She authorized me," Sullivan was saying. "Send a man down to the HQ to ask."

"I believe you, but I've got to get Colonel Thatcher's okay before I let anyone out of the compound except for target practice. We're expecting a patrol to come back in a few days. When they come, you might get permission to go out as their replacement."

"I'm not going out for that kind of exercise," Sullivan said.

"I'll need an okay from Colonel—"

"I know the reason you want to keep them here," Sullivan said, making sure he said it loud enough for the Arabs behind him to hear clearly. All of them spoke at least rudimentary English.

"What do you mean?" Bronnard was scowling in puzzlement now.

"Why do you play the waiting game with them? Why don't you simply kill them now?"

"I don't know what you're talking about."

"I'm serving notice now. I sympathize with these men. Their cause means something to me. I'm not going to let anything happen to them. You can tell Arafat that yourself."

"Listen," Bronnard growled, "around here we don't talk politics, we talk ordnance and—"

"Yeah, I guess it's something you'd rather not talk about." He reached down and pushed open the gate—and froze.

Bronnard had stuck the barrel of his Skorpion machine pistol in Sullivan's ribs. "Take your fucking hands off that gate."

"Stop it, Captain. Lower the gun." Tora's voice. Bronnard looked past Sullivan's shoulder at her.

For a moment Sullivan was sure Bronnard would deny her.

"Yeah. Sure. But when your father shapes up—"

"I'll take responsibility. Back off, Captain Bronnard."

Bronnard lowered the gun and backpedaled.

"Go on, Mr. Stark," she said.

"You're making a mistake, letting that guy take over. He's up to something," Bronnard blurted.

Tora said nothing. Sullivan glanced over his shoulder at her and was surprised to see her holding a .45 pistol on Bronnard.

Sullivan shrugged and led his six men through the gate and into the woods.

After they'd gone a few hundred yards, El-Mahud trotted up beside Sullivan, his M16 clacking against his bandoliers, darkness and light alternating on his intense boyish face as they passed in and out of the shade of the trees. "What did you mean about the 'reason you want to keep us here' when you spoke to that man Bronnard?" he demanded.

Sullivan shook his head. "He was right. We shouldn't talk politics. I should stay out of it."

"But you said something about Arafat. What has Arafat got to do with us here? He is not one of us. The PLO are cowards and weaklings who negotiate with Jews. They are our enemies."

"You're not supposed to talk on an exercise unless given permission."

"I must know! I told our major we should not trust this camp. It must be CIA—it's in America. But he said . . ." He broke off, scowling. "Why do you laugh?"

"CIA! Nothing like it. The CIA would kill everyone who works here. No. I shouldn't have shot off my mouth. Forget it. Get back in line."

El-Mahud did as he was told.

But Sullivan knew the young terrorist would be thinking, and thinking. And brooding.

"Whenever possible," Sullivan told them, "the sentries to be removed should be observed from a distance for one full day so their movement patterns can be taken into account, as well as the nature of the approach areas. This is of course particularly relevant to *stealthy* sentry removal. Without guns. For example—is the sentry right- or left-handed? Is he wearing heavy or light clothing? To which direction does he tend to pay most attention? Over what type of surface will the final approach be made?"

It was just after noon. They'd had their rations and their rest.

They were sitting in a small clearing in a circle around Sullivan, and he felt absurdly like a scoutmaster explaining knots to a group of attentive Boy Scouts—teaching bloodthirsty Boy Scouts the best way to kill a sentry. . . .

"A right-handed sentry reacts to a surprise attack with his right hand, and, given a choice, turns clockwise to face an attack from the rear." Sullivan paused to glance at his watch. It would be time to move on soon, to the "surprise party." But until that moment came, it would be necessary for him to stay in character.

All during the lecture, one part of his mind was going over the files Tora had shown him, comparing the file information to the living counterparts before him. The assessments, psychological and cultural, seemed correct. But the files had been in code—she'd had to read them to him, decoding as she went. He hadn't yet pressed her to give him the decoding formula. He could open the files—but he couldn't read them without her help. It was too soon to ask her for it. So he hadn't seen the file on Jack Sullivan.

". . . at first contact with the sentry, when approaching from behind," Sullivan was saying, "cross-grab the right-rear quarter of the sentry's head and jerk it down and around at a forty-degree angle, step under the direction of the target's fall, with your other hand bringing the blade up against the carotid artery, which should be exposed if you've . . ."

He broke off, listening.

Someone was coming through the brush. Stealthily.

Sullivan had a pretty good idea who it would be.

He moved so that the group of trainees were between him and the woods through which his stalker approached. The trainees were rubbernecking to follow Sullivan's movements. Sullivan was saying, "You two—El-Mahud, Ahmed—come with me. The rest of you take positions at four places around the clearing. You are standing sentry. We'll dry-run a hit. Don't get trigger-happy with us. . . ." Sullivan led El-Mahud and Ahmed into the woods. "Move as quietly as you can," he instructed them. "Stay low—we'll act as if there's a fifth instructor in the woods . . ."

He led them in a zigzag run through a stand of pitch-redolent Douglas firs. He paused beside a lightning-blasted tree trunk, recently fallen. He ducked low behind it, and a moment later one of the smaller, needle-tufted branches upthrusting from the trunk sagged over, shot through at its base by a heavy-caliber attack rifle. A second later Sullivan heard the rolling boom of the shot.

El-Mahud and Ahmed looked at him wide-eyed. "The fools are firing at us!" Ahmed blurted.

"No," El-Mahud observed, "that wasn't our kind of rifle."

"Very good," Sullivan remarked dryly. "That was a Browning assault rifle, I think. Bronnard probably went to get the proper weapon for a long-distance shot before he came after us. And he has a talent for tracking, that man."

"How do you know it's Captain Bronnard?" El-Mahud asked. "And why?"

"Oh, I've been expecting Captain Bronnard." He had been half-expecting Bronnard to jump him, in fact. Bronnard was afraid he'd take control of the camp away from him. Probably Bronnard planned to kill him and the others, hide the bodies, claim that they'd simply disappeared.

But to El-Mahud he said, "Why does he want to kill *you*? Isn't it obvious?"

"Me? He's after *me*?"

"He's after the PFLP . . . Keep down!"

The heavy-gauge ammo chewed away more of the bark on the tree as the Arab risked a look. El-Mahud ducked his head back down.

"He is . . ." Ahmed broke off to mutter something in Arabic as they heard shouting from the clearing. The other Arabs were shouting questions. Sullivan hoped they'd taken cover. Their time wasn't yet. "He is an Israeli sympathizer?"

"Part of the Zionist conspiracy," Sullivan confirmed, hoping the absurd lie sounded convincing.

"I knew it," El-Mahud growled. "An evil-looking man."

"Wait here," Sullivan said. "Stay down. If you hear me shout, give me some suppressive fire—but don't move from your position."

Sullivan wormed ahead through the short grass, dragging himself along on his elbows, his M16 loose on its shoulder strap, diagonal across his back.

He came to a place where the tree trunk had humped in a low arch over the grass. Looking through the arch, he glimpsed the blurred outline of a gunman dashing from one clump of trees to another.

"Thirty degrees to the northeast!" Sullivan shouted. "Suppressive!"

El-Mahud shouted an oath in Arabic and popped up, M16 against his shoulder, spraying three long bursts into the clump of trees shielding Bronnard. At the same time, Sullivan leaped up, vaulted the log, and churned into the woods, dodging as he went. The tree trunks here were clouded with blackberry bushes, the berries heavy on the vine, ripe and leaking bloodred juice. Sullivan knelt under cover of one green-and-black-red tangle, rifle in hand now. The firing had stopped. The woods were eerily quiet.

There was a lot of ground cover between him and Bronnard, and both men were experienced jungle fighters—they could go round and round here, neither one gaining an advantage until one or the other got lucky. Luck could be treacherous.

Sullivan believed in covering his bets.

There was a thick, squat fir tree, its upper half splintered by lightning, between Sullivan and Bronnard's position. Sullivan decided to take a chance on exposing himself for a moment in order to get a strategic advantage.

He slung the rifle over his shoulder . . . and climbed a tree.

The horny bark, sticky with patches of amber pitch, offered plenty of lifesaving handholds. Lifesaving, because it was a question of speed. He had to get into firing position before Bronnard spotted him on the tree. The trunk offered partial cover, but Bronnard might get a clear shot at him in the gaps between its outbranchings.

Sullivan wedged himself into a branching crotch about twenty-five feet up, squinting against the sun to search for Bronnard, at the same time unslinging his rifle.

He could see the two Arabs in their gray fatigues sprawled behind the fallen tree trunk, about twenty yards away. Beyond, he caught a flicker of movement from the clearing. He could just make out four figures in gray stupidly crowded together behind a bush there. Thinking they were taking cover, but all the time easier targets by reason of staying together.

Another flicker of motion—Bronnard, moving in on El-Mahud and Ahmed.

Bronnard was coming at them from behind, only thirty feet off, raising his rifle to fire.

"Sorry, Bronnard," Sullivan muttered. "I'm gonna need those creeps."

He had the M16 nocked between two antlerlike branches, like a firing tripod. The shooting angle was uncomfortable—he was straddling the tree crotch, firing sideways, at a ninety-degree angle from his frame, like an Indian shooting from horseback.

The M16 bucked in Sullivan's hands; ejected shells arced to his right and plinked off the tree branches.

A flock of birds, startled, lifted off in a fluttery cloud.

Bronnard staggered and let his rifle slip from his fingers. He looked up at Sullivan, shook his head once as their eyes locked. And then he fell.

Sullivan felt a tug of regret. Bronnard had been a collaborator with terrorists, totally amoral—but he was also a warrior, a soldier of fortune, not so different from Sullivan himself.

Sullivan shouldered the rifle and climbed down off the tree. The pitch on his hands made him curse—it made him angrier than it should have.

He jogged through the trees, kicking angrily at snagging blackberry vines.

When he got to the glade where Bronnard had fallen, he wasn't there.

The Arabs had gone on to the other side of the fallen tree. They peered over it at him like nature spirits, their faces exotic and dark. "Keep down," Sullivan said, crouching.

He saw the depression in the knee-high grass and ferns where Bronnard had fallen. A trail of slick red led to a hump of blackberry bushes. Bronnard's assault rifle was gone.

Sullivan threw himself flat—and steel-jacketed murder cut the air where he'd stood a moment before. He heard the multiple boom of the automatic rifle. Blue gunsmoke drifted up from the tangle of vines twenty feet to his left. Bronnard was near.

Sullivan dragged the rifle free and crept through the grass to flank Bronnard. He expected to be shot at again, but there was no sound or motion from the bushes.

Sullivan gained the shelter of a pine that seemed to be bowing, bent over at the middle by another fallen tree. He raised up enough to peer through the sticky green branches. He could see sun-glint on gunmetal—he knew the way light on a gun barrel looked—through a break in the vines. The vines shivered . . . and Bronnard came into view.

He was on his knees, holding on to the rifle as if it were a crutch, swaying.

Sullivan moved out from shelter, keeping the M16 leveled on Bronnard.

Bronnard turned to look dully at him as he approached. He made no move to fight. He stared, his mirror glasses gone, his noseless, ravaged face looking more than ever that of a dead man.

In seconds, Sullivan stood over him.

Bronnard's belly had been shot open; he clutched yards of bloodied intestine in his right hand, instinctively protective.

"We all loved her," Bronnard said. "I loved her too, even after she shot my face away. I stayed, even after that. That's how much I loved her. Now you're going to—"

Sullivan squeezed the trigger and erased Bronnard from this world, breaking his skull apart with a burst from the M16.

He turned away, haunted by Bronnard's words, thinking: She did that to him. Shot his face away. She's more a monster than I knew. A monster I make love to.

"We go back to the camp now, I think," El-Mahud said grimly, getting up as Sullivan approached.

Sullivan shook his head. "Not directly. Wouldn't be safe. We'll have to circle around the long way. Follow me."

12
Setting Up the Toy Soldiers

It felt strange wearing a dead man's uniform. Snag didn't like it. He didn't buy the religion of his forefathers. But Indians don't feel right about disturbing the dead—particularly about taking their clothing from them and putting it on. The spirits would assume he was willing to go to the Land of the Dead in place of the dead man. . . .

Snag chuckled and shook his head.

He was already in the Land of the Dead.

He sat propped against a sun-washed boulder, his assault rifle across his knees, gazing across the ravine toward the pine woods on the far side. Absently he fingered the bullet holes, edged with dried blood, on the appropriated gray fatigues he wore.

It hadn't been pleasant, skinning the uniforms from the dead men.

He hand-rolled a cigarette with Top tobacco taken from a beaded deerskin pouch, his only concession to Indian culture, and lit it with a Bic butane lighter.

He stuck the cigarette in his lips—and it dropped from his slack lips as he stiffened, listening hard. The scrape of footsteps somewhere behind him.

There were a lot of sounds on the edge of the ravine that afternoon. There were faint whistles of wind, the rhythmic squeaking of insects, the cries of birds. The footsteps were very faint, and someone else might have mistaken them for the rattle of sliding rocks. But Snag's Indian heritage was more intact in him than he knew.

Snag moved noiselessly around the big boulder. It was poised almost on the edge of the ravine, with a two-foot ledge of rock beneath it. He sidled around the boulder, his back to empty space, came out on the other side, and slunk up behind the big man in gray fatigues and black beret crouching there, a yard off.

Snag cocked his rifle and prepared to kill the man . . .

. . . who spun and launched himself at the Indian, knocking the gun aside and barreling into his knees, taking him down in a football tackle. Then they were rolling over and over, coating in dust, to the edge of the ravine, rocking there, both about to tumble over, arms entwined. They looked each other in the face.

"Sullivan!"

Sullivan grunted and pulled free, getting to his feet. He bent and helped Snag up. Sullivan grinned. "You're pretty good."

"Why the hell did you—?"

"I couldn't see you clearly from below. I didn't know it was you, for sure. Where's Rolff and Merlin?"

"Up the hill, in position. I'm supposed to be standing lookout." He looked around. "Where are the—?"

"Waiting for me in the woods. I just wanted to see if everything was ready. Tell Rolff and Merlin: no more than two. Preferably only one."

He clapped Snag on the back. "*Damn,* you've got good ears!" And he turned to make his way down the trail that led across the ravine.

Dave Moran and Bud Hauser sat in Moran's racing-striped blue-and-silver GMC pickup, drinking boilermakers and watching the Riverbend Motel. Hauser's left arm was in a cast and a sling. Moran's left hand was bound up for its two broken middle fingers. His ribs, under his red plaid shirt, were taped up on the right side; a swatch of bandage tape covered his nose in a triangle of white.

"That nigger's been in there with that bitch for a long time," Hauser growled. He wedged a plastic Budweiser cup between his legs on the seat behind the steering wheel and refilled it from a quart bottle, leaving just enough room for a healthy shot of J&B. A boilermaker.

"Fine white girl like that," Moran muttered. "Not only consorting with niggers, but *foreign* niggers."

"They got niggers on TV," Hauser said, "and all kinds of sex stuff that makes a decent man sick. But they never have no interracial couples. You notice that? Even TV wouldn't sink that low. Nobody sinks that low."

"You think she's screwin' that jigaboo?"

"What else?"

"I think she's wet for that scar-face son of a bitch. Stark, his name is. She's hanging out here waiting for him."

"I don't know. She looked awful friendly with that nigger."

"I'd hate to believe that a fine white girl like that . . ." Moran shook his head. "Bad example."

"We got to do something about that."

"Something sure gotta be done."

Sullivan stood up and checked the sun. It was on the verge of sinking behind the mountains.

He nodded to himself. It was time.

Ahmed and El-Mahud were arguing in their own language. Sullivan asked, "What's the problem?"

Young El-Mahud shrugged. "Ahmed thinks we're making a mistake if we mobilize, like you say—he says if we attack the camp, we'll only get killed and it will be a great waste of PFLP force."

130

Ahmed interrupted. "We don't know enough to take such a step! Maybe this Bronnard was acting alone. We have sworn to say nothing of politics, to finish our training . . ."

Ahmed was bigger than the others, his skin a shade lighter, his accent not so thick. Perhaps he'd been educated in London—ideologically sympathetic but just discovering he had no stomach for the necessity of violence.

"What do you think the Jews are up to?" Sullivan asked him quietly. "Do you think this Bronnard could be working alone? Do the Jews ever work alone? They are conspirers."

"Yes, but—"

"Are you afraid of them too, El-Mahud?" Sullivan demanded.

The smaller Arab threw him a glare. "Afraid? I know what must be done, and I'll do it! The Jews have pushed us out of our homeland and we will take it back no matter what the cost. I am afraid of nothing! Even the ugly tasks—I do them with pride! My brother killed a family of Jews—he burned them alive to make an example! I would do the same! I would die, I would—"

The others drowned him out in a chorus of agreement.

All except Ahmed, who looked decidedly worried.

"I have always hated the Jews," Sullivan said. Nothing could be a bigger lie—Lily had been Jewish, and he had been close to her family. He'd worked for Israeli intelligence for two years, and not for the money alone. "The Jews, the Zionists, are trying to control the world. I have spent time in Palestine . . . or what was *once* Palestine . . ." He went on to speak nostalgically of time spent with Arab friends in Palestine. And this part was true—these Arabs had not been terrorists. They believed in a Palestinian state, but they favored achieving it through political negotiation. Sullivan left out this last detail.

Sullivan concluded, looking at Ahmed, "The Arafat faction is simply interested in the conflict because it makes money on agenting arms sales to PLO units. It is in its interests to prolong the conflict, so they deliberately sabotage those who would act drastically. They are out to destroy you. Give in to them or fight them—they are here at the camp. Let them butcher you like sheep if you want."

"We will fight them here!" cried El-Mahud.

"It may be necessary," Sullivan said, looking hard at Ahmed, "to eliminate anyone who collaborates with the tainted faction."

All five of the other Arabs turned to look at Ahmed.

"I am with you," Ahmed said after a moment. "All the way."

The darkness was nearly upon them.

The wall of the ravine was here split by a V-shaped crevice. A faint trail led through the crevice, down the hillside, and across the ravine.

"Let's go!" Sullivan shouted. "Quick, before it's too dark to see!"

The six terrorists filed through the crevice and down the path into the ravine, into the deepening shadows.

The terrorists were superficially convinced that a "conspiracy" was working against them at the camp. But Sullivan knew that when it came to convincing the others of their faction to take up arms against the rest of the camp, El-Mahud and companions would need total indoctrination. There must be no shadow of a doubt. And so the toy soldiers had to be set up.

Sullivan let them get nearly to the top of the far side of the ravine before raising his lighter, flicking its flame three times to give Rolff the signal. Almost immediately, his signal was answered by gunshots. He saw muzzle flashes against the patchy wall of dark blue and gray and heard a shrill scream.

He moved cautiously down into the ravine, took cover behind a boulder when stray AK47 rounds kicked up the dirt at his feet.

If he wasn't careful, he realized, he could be killed by his own setup.

A lull in the shooting came; the ravine echoed with the final shots and went back to its ancient, primordial silence.

"El-Muhad!" Sullivan shouted. "Ahmed! Bruhol! Retreat! *Retreat!*"

The gunfire recommenced, bullets ricocheting through the boulders.

Sullivan aimed his M16 at a boulder on the face of the cliff near the clash point where the Arabs were flattened down by fire from above. He was careful to aim at a place that would harmlessly absorb fire, so he didn't risk hitting his own men. His own men being Rolff, Merlin, and Snag.

Under cover of this false "suppressive fire," Ahmed, El-Mahud, and others returned, churning up the dust, eyes wild, faces shiny with sweat in the last rays of the sun reflected from the rocks overhead.

"Where's Bruhol?" Sullivan asked.

"Shot down!" said El-Mahud breathlessly, taking cover behind the boulder. "Men from the camp—they had the camp uniforms! They tried to kill us all!"

"You were right!" another blurted. "A conspiracy! Arafat's murderers!"

Sullivan looked at Ahmed, and was surprised by his expression. He was staring at Sullivan, breathing hard.

Sullivan took command. "Go, keep going, back up the hill! I'll cover you!"

They ran, and Sullivan pretended to fire at the "Arafat conspiracy," which pretended to return fire, shooting over the heads of the men running up the trail.

Sullivan followed, now and then turning to spray bursts either too low or too high to hit his own men.

They regrouped in the woods, cursing and puffing, Sullivan doing his best to appear as outraged and shaken up as the Arabs.

"Do you think they'll follow us?" El-Mahud asked.

Sullivan shook his head.

"You seem quite sure of that," said Ahmed levelly.

Sullivan looked hard at him. This time Ahmed didn't shrink back. Sullivan shrugged and said, "They were firing at us from a position of strength up there. Here we could ambush them. They'll regroup with others first, and that'll take time."

El-Mahud said, "I heard one of them shout, 'Cut the Palestinians down before they can retreat!'"

Sullivan raised an eyebrow. Merlin, it seemed, was getting too fancy. Still, the Arabs seemed to have bought it. When you get men stirred up, afraid or angry, boiling with adrenaline, they'll believe almost anything that feeds their paranoia.

Ahmed surprised Sullivan by saying, "Maybe you and I should check out the trail behind us, just to make sure they aren't following."

Sullivan shrugged. "Why not? Come on—you four rest, but stay alert. Keep a sharp watch. We'll be back in a few minutes."

He led Ahmed back the way they had come, through the woods. It was dark now, the only light starlight and moonlight. The two men were just silhouettes and metal glints to one another when they paused, out of sight of the rest camp, on the far side of a sprawling berry bush and a thatch of close-set trees. Sullivan turned to Ahmed and said, "Spit it out. What is it you want to talk to me about in private?"

But Ahmed had his M16 pointed at Sullivan's belly. It was nearly point-blank range.

Sullivan's own rifle was slung over his shoulder. His only defense now was his brain and his voice. "Ahmed—"

"Who the hell are you?" Ahmed demanded.

His Arabic accent had vanished.

Sullivan hesitated. "It seems I ought to ask you the same thing. Who the hell are *you*?"

"My name is Knickian. Department of Defense Intelligence Agency."

"DIA?" The Pentagon's own intelligence service. "How long have you people known about the camp?"

"Only a few months—and we've only learned that it was in the USA in the last few weeks. It was a shock when they brought me *here*—I thought we were heading for Libya."

"Knickian. . . . Armenian?"

"Uh-huh."

"A mole in the Palestinian—"

"Obviously. Now who the fuck are you?"

Some instinct told Sullivan to opt for the truth. "My enemies are yours also. I'm here to kill them—they killed someone close to me."

"Here to . . . Are you kidding? There's forty of them!"

"Forty-one, I think. I'm not alone. There are three others."

"The three who sprang that fake ambush on us?"

"That's right. We've already accounted for fourteen or so—"

"Dammit! Do you know what those dead men

135

could have meant to us in terms of intelligence sources?"

"They're fanatics. They wouldn't have talked. Anyway, the government has shown again and again it can't be trusted to do an effective job against terrorism. So now the rest of us have to do it our way. But don't think I'm not gathering intelligence. I may have access to their files—"

"They keep files?"

"In code. I . . ." Sullivan suddenly realized he didn't know enough about this Knickian. "How do I know you're . . . ?"

Knickian slowly lowered the gun. He looked around, then bent and took off his shoe. He bent the lining of the sole up, and from a hollow heel took out a folded photostat. Sullivan lit his lighter to read it. I.D. for the DIA.

He passed it back. The important thing, really, was that the guy *felt* right.

Okay. He was a fed. But he was still in the way.

"So what the hell are you up to?" Knickian demanded. "I mean, it looks like you think you're going to turn these people against one another. Right?"

Sullivan said nothing.

"That's what I thought. Look, man . . . you've accounted for a lot of them. Get the hell out and leave it to us. We'll take your vengeance for you. Leave it to the professionals."

Sullivan had to laugh. "Professionals!"

"Okay, you're a professional merc. But—"

"I'm a professional taker of vengeance, Knickian," Sullivan said quietly. "You might say I'm a specialist in it."

There was a moment or two when the two men were quiet, listening to the crickets, the swish of wind in the trees. It was getting chilly, and damp.

And then Knickian burst out, "You're the Specialist! Jack Sullivan, right?"

"Keep your voice down, Agent 452."

"Did I guess it or not?"

"Yeah. Now shut up about it."

Knickian had raised the rifle again. "You're too dangerous, man. I've been hearing about you for . . . Yeah, you might just get away with it. You might just kill them all, from what I've heard. But if you do that, you're blowing it for us. This place is a key to all the underground channels of international terrorism. We need these assholes alive."

"I'll get the files to you. But the Blue Man and the Nine are going to die, Knickian."

"I can't let you do it."

"What are you going to do about it? You going to kill me? Shoot me down in cold blood? That what you want?"

Sullivan had heard admiration in Knickian's voice when he'd said "The Specialist." He knew Knickian didn't want to kill him.

"No," Knickian admitted. "But I don't know what else to do without jeopardizing my mission. I worked for years getting into this, Sullivan."

"Maybe, just maybe, if you give me the straight line on your timetable, I'll cooperate with you and back off."

"What timetable?"

"The raid. The DIA's going to come down on these creeps, isn't it?"

Knickian sounded a little embarrassed now. It was Knickian who held the gun on Sullivan, but it was also Knickian who was defensive. "Sure—they'll raid them. But we don't want to blow it by coming in too soon. It's got to be done carefully."

Sullivan snorted derisively. "They're moving out soon. Tora told me. By the time you people move in, the place'll be deserted. And if your people come in sooner, they'll alert them. You can't bring a big force like that in here without warning the Blue Man's people. They'll see it coming. He must have a dozen ways out. All the important ones will get away. My way, none of them will escape. Because we'll come down on them from within and from without at once. And you're coming to kill, not to capture. That 'take-them-prisoner' routine will cripple you."

"That's your theory."

But Knickian was troubled, and that meant he was distracted. That made it a good time for Sullivan to make his move.

He clapped his hands on the gun barrel a few inches from his belly, gripped it, and yanked with all his strength. It came easily from the startled Knickian's grasp. Before the man could shout or make a move, Sullivan gave the rifle back to him—in the jaw, smashing him with the gun butt.

Knickian toppled over backward, out cold.

Sullivan stared down at the dark figure on the ground. "Always complications," he muttered. Then he reversed the rifle in his hands. What the hell else could he do with the man? He cocked the gun and aimed it at the fallen man's head.

No. He couldn't kill him. No matter how important the mission was. But what, then?

Five minutes later El-Mahud and the other Arabs jumped to their feet, alert.

They'd heard gunshots in the woods.

13

The Wild Card Is Dealt

When Sullivan returned to the rest camp alone, El-Mahud demanded, "Where is Ahmed?"

Sullivan shook his head sadly. "He didn't listen to me. He ran off down the trail and out into the open—by the ravine. He wanted to avenge Bruhol. One of their snipers got him. Right between the eyes."

The remaining Arabs gabbled excitedly to one another.

"Come on," Sullivan said. "Let's get the hell out of here. We'll march for an hour or so, put some distance between us and them."

"But now we go . . . where?"

"Back to the camp. I'll get you to your friends safely. Leave it to me."

He led them into the thickening darkness along a trail showing like a snail track in the pale light filtering down through the trees.

Sullivan was thinking about the mission, and wishing to God he hadn't had to undertake it by infiltration. It wasn't good to see the men you had to kill this closely, this personally.

Still, they were terrorists. They were for real. He had heard them speak reverently of strikes made by their friends. Strikes? Bombings in restaurants, bus stations, hotels, embassies—the butchering of innocents.

It was necessary to make a point, they said. Only by making your presence felt with terror could you force the world to listen to your demands, when you were so outnumbered. But Sullivan could not think of a time when terrorism had actually worked. Not in any deeply significant way. It had worked to terrorize—but the terror had done nothing for the political ideas it was alleged to represent. Nothing had been accomplished except an inflaming of hatreds that ended in the slaughter of the very people the terrorism was supposed to benefit—like the murder of innocent Palestinian refugees at the hands of the "Christian" Phalangists in Beirut. All those little children shot to pieces—victims of their own freedom fighters, in a roundabout way, as much as of the men who'd actually pulled the triggers. They'd been caught in the vicious circle of terror.

And it was clear that all the men in training at the camp were eager to fuel that fire. They would never be persuaded from it. There was no hope in reasoning with them. They were either totally fanatic or totally self-serving, hoping that it would make riches for them as it had for Carlos and the others who dealt in arms and ransoms and extortions. Certain people had made a lot of money on terrorism. They'd also made a big mistake. They'd killed Jack Sullivan's Lily.

Sullivan knew that the time of full and complete reckoning was near. He could feel it.

All the elements were combining properly, all the pieces falling together. Knickian had been a temporary complication. But now that was all over. . . .

George Knickian woke hearing five brass bands all playing different songs—and playing them badly.

For a while he tried to sort them out. Then he realized that his ears were ringing, and his head

140

buzzing, and that he was still caught up in some mad dream. He forced himself to sit up, and his head was cleared by a lightning flash of pain. The brass bands departed, the pain stayed.

He looked muzzily around him.

He seemed to be in a sort of grotto, the floor bubbling like an immense caldron, the air murky with steam smelling of sulfur. The light came from a Coleman lantern against the water-beaded rock wall. Four men sat around the lantern, smoking, watching him. Men in gray fatigues. One looked like an Indian. There was a heavyset older guy, always quiet. Another was long and thin, with a sardonic expression; the fourth looked coldly Teutonic. The thin one nodded at him. "How you feel pal?"

Knickian winced, then said, "Rotten. Head hurts. Jaw sore. Wrists in pain."

"The boss had to tie your wrists. I'll cut you loose—but you got to promise to be good."

The German looked at the thin one in surprise. "A promise? He is a Boy Scout?"

The thin one chuckled. "He's an agent for the DIA. But I'm not going to trust his promise completely. We'll guarantee he keeps it. We'll stand watches."

The Indian stood, and walking bent over under the rock overhang, came at him with a knife.

For a moment he was sure they intended to kill him, that the remarks about cutting him loose had been a mockery. But then the Indian turned him on his side and cut the ropes away.

The Indian backed off, and Knickian stretched a little, massaging his wrists. "I guess I better make myself more comfortable," he said. "I take it I'm gonna be here awhile."

The thin one grinned. "You got it right, pal. We'll

141

probably have to truss you up and leave you here awhile tomorrow."

"Yeah? Why?"

"We'll have some work to do." He patted the Uzi machine pistol on the sleeping bag beside him. All three men had formidable weapons within reach— and well out of Knickian's reach.

The Indian brought him a bowl of hot freeze-dried vegetable soup. He ate gratefully. When he finished, he said, "You know, you guys seem pretty decent. You know who I am. You know why I'm here. Listen, you know, too, I guess, that you're in trouble. You're carrying illegal weapons, and you're using them on people without authorization. But if you cooperate with me, I'm pretty sure I can get you off—"

He broke off, annoyed by their laughter.

After they'd quieted, Birdwell said, "Even if we were ready to help you, it'd be crazy to cross the Specialist."

Merlin shook his head. "He wouldn't kill us for going to the cops. He doesn't gun anybody who doesn't deserve it bad. But I wouldn't want to be known as the guy who'd betrayed him. The Specialist is . . ." He smiled. "Something special."

"I signed on for the duration," said the Indian darkly. "No matter what."

Knickian shrugged. "I had to have a shot at it. . . . So, you're the guys who were shooting at me a few hours back. Sullivan brought me here, told you who I was, that I knew who he was, what I'm—"

"The whole dirty tale," Merlin confirmed. "Damn government agents getting underfoot when decent law-abiding mercenaries are trying to get some serious killing done."

Rolff grunted in something like laughter. Gallows humor appealed to him.

"You guys got any more of that soup? . . . Thanks."

After he ate, he lay back and muttered, "The hell with it, I'm gonna catch some Z's."

He closed his eyes and dozed, but didn't allow himself to sleep.

He waited.

Malta was having a strange dream. A dream of his childhood.

He was a small boy again, in Ethiopia, in his uncle's grand house. He heard his father telling his uncle that the guerrillas were moving in, and how he was going to take his family to Algeria.

His uncle was telling his father, "You must be mad! To live among the Arabs?"

And then the dream jumped ahead to Algeria, the screams as his parents were killed by the assassins who'd come from Ethiopia for that purpose alone. . . . And the boy had run into the streets, to begin his life as a thief. . . .

He seemed to see himself, seven years old, learning to pick pockets. He was reaching into a tall man's pocket. But the man turned and caught his arm. Young Malta screamed and tried to get away —he looked up into the man's eyes, and saw that it was his father. With a bullet-hole in his black forehead. "It's all right, son! It's all right! But don't take from the woman! Because there is death in her purse!" The boy looked at the woman his father pointed to. A slender blond woman with laughing blue eyes.

Angie.

Malta woke, sat up on the bed, sweating, and cleared the mist from his eyes with a sharp shake of his head. He looked at the softly breathing, curvaceous figure beside him on the bed. Her blond hair

143

lay in pleasantly chaotic tangles across the white pillow. Her blue eyes were closed.

Angie. The waitress at the Elkhorn. She'd been renting a cabin at the Riverbend Motel herself. They'd begun to talk, and she'd invited him in for a meal. She listened with fascination as he talked about his childhood—and for his part, he was astonished that he *was* talking about it.

But there was something infinitely gentle about her, something both country-naive and earthily wise, and he knew that he could trust her. Still, he told her nothing of the mission. He spoke vaguely of his friends being here for a fishing trip, and then he'd looked at her apologetically, and she'd understood that he'd lied to her only because he had to.

"You know," she'd said once, "we're a scandal around here."

"I know, my golden one. I was surprised when you . . ."

She blushed, and it was a beautiful thing to see, that blush, like the first ruddy glows of a sunset. "I've always been attracted to black men. And you looked like you . . . Like royalty."

He'd been pleased with that. His family had been of the Ethiopian royalty. His first family. He'd been adopted by a Algerian and raised as an Algerian.

She stirred, and after a moment sat up. "What time is it?" she asked sleepily.

"I don't know, my dear," Malta said gently. "Best you go back to sleep."

"I can't. Not until . . . I had a dream about you." She rubbed her soft round cheek against his shoulder. "A real nice dream."

He took her in his arms.

Much later, he lay unable to sleep, one arm thrown around her. Her breasts rose and fell rhythmically with her breathing, so that they seemed to nuzzle his biceps.

He was almost asleep when he heard a faint scraping from the window. He lay very still, listening. The sound wasn't repeated.

The room was dim. The only light came through the bathroom door, indirectly. He'd forgotten to turn off the bathroom light.

He peered at the four-paned square window. There was something just visible through the dingy glass . . . something that shouldn't be there. A man's face, with a bandage where the nose should be.

It was a face Malta recognized.

He reached under the pillow for the gun.

It wasn't there.

And then he remembered that he'd hidden it somewhere else because he hadn't wanted it to frighten Angie. His brain was cobwebbed with sleepiness. Where was the gun?

Malta eased away from Angie, and pretending to move in his sleep, as if unconsciously seeking more comfort, he turned over and let his arm flop over the edge of the mattress. He felt under the bed. There. The lump under the rug. A flat, squarish .45.

He clawed at it—and accidentally pushed it farther away.

A rattle from the door.

What was it she'd said? *You know, we're a scandal around here.*

His groping fingers closed around the gun. He heard the door open, felt the cold air rush into the room, coming before the killers as if it were a servant arriving early to announce the coming of death.

Malta knew that death was very close. The cold

145

air brought goose bumps out on his arms as he sat up and leveled the gun at the doorway.

The door was open. But there was no one there.

The window shattered inward, and he turned too late to see who was shooting at him. He felt the bullet strike his chest at the same moment he saw the muzzle flash, and as the room sank around him he heard Angie scream.

14

The Parade Ground and the Killing Ground

Snag was wondering again.

He was wondering if maybe the DIA man was right. But he knew that even if he was right, and they were all doomed because of what they were doing, he would stay the course with Sullivan. Sitting around the Coleman lantern waiting for Sullivan, Merlin had begun to tell him stories. Stories about Jack Sullivan. Merlin had said, "You've got a right to know who he is, since you're fighting for him. And you just might get killed fighting for him." After hearing a few of the stories, Snag had realized that he had heard about Sullivan before—only he had been called the Specialist in the stories Snag had heard.

One of the stories had to do with the way the Specialist had gotten his nickname. It was in Vietnam. Every so often the C.O. would come and ask for volunteers for dangerous solo jobs. Sullivan always volunteered, saying, "You need a man to do a missile-launcher hit on a munitions dump? It just happens that missile launchers are my specialty." If the C.O. needed a man who could work out of helicopters, Sullivan would insist he could do it because helicopters were his specialty. Sniping? That was his specialty. He almost always achieved what he set out to do, and one day he stepped forward to volunteer and the C.O. said, "Here he comes again. The Specialist."

Real dry, like he was making a joke of it.

And everyone laughed.

The C.O. said, "Sullivan, dammit, is there anything you don't specialize in?"

And Sullivan replied, "I only specialize in one thing, to be truthful, sir."

"What's that?"

"Killing the enemy."

And no one laughed. Because it was true.

Just after that, Sullivan had been made chief of long-range reconnaissance patrols. Lurps were the most daring, gonzo infantrymen in the war. Their missions were nearly always suicidal. But when they went out under the Specialist, most of them came back.

After the war, the nom de guerre had remained with Sullivan, only now it was said he specialized in something more . . . well, more specialized.

He specialized in revenge.

Anyone who had a just case for revenge, whose family or friends had been killed or crippled by the legions of madmen, terrorists, thugs, mobsters, or psycho killers roaming the world, could set his case in front of the Specialist. If you convinced him it was on the level, if his investigation showed that you were telling the truth, and if you deserved redress, he got it for you. He had a talent, it was said, for empathy, for understanding how you felt about the horror that had been done to you. He had a special sympathy for the victims of the world, a sense of their helplessness, an identification with their frustration, and a burning desire to set things straight for them. Your own thirst for revenge became his. He became the living instrument of your desire for justice. And damn the legality.

148

Sure, it was said he charged big fees. But there were also stories of his doing it for nothing, if he felt the cause was especially right.

It was said he could see evil in a man the way an X ray sees a tumor, as if he had an almost supernatural ability to look into you and recognize it. A talent for knowing who was guilty, irrevocably guilty, and who wasn't.

It was said he'd killed many men—and, by some miracle, every one of them had deserved it.

Still, Snag sat beside the glowing Coleman lantern, watching the water bubble in the hot springs beside him, listening to the regular breathing of the other four men—the three mercenaries and their prisoner—and wondering, wondering, if Sullivan were truly infallible. Wondering if he were doing the right thing in following him.

But the bottom line was this: all through life a man had doubts, wondering, wondering, if he were taking the right course. And yet he followed his instincts and his hunches and he kept right on, doing what he felt, what he knew he had to do, and all the wondering didn't count for jackshit in the end. A man just did things the best way he knew how.

Snag was a little sleepy, and deeply immersed in his thinking, and so he didn't notice it when Knickian moved very slowly, achingly slowly, to his knees and gathered himself up for a spring at Snag.

He didn't notice it till Knickian was ready to spring.

Snag swore and brought the rifle around—but it was too late.

Knickian hit him hard, before Snag was quite on his feet, catching him off balance. The two men

149

rolled, struggling, past the lip of the bubbling crater and down the rocky hillside.

The starry sky spun for Snag, and he had a whirling glimpse of the DIA agent's contorted face, and then all the stars seemed to fall from the sky and fly into his eyes. He'd hit his head on a rock. He heard shouting, and gunfire, but he was too stunned to move.

Someone was shaking his arm. Snag forced himself to sit up. His head throbbed. "Where is he?" he asked, wincing at the pain brought by speaking.

"He got away," Merlin said flatly.

Snag thought: I've blown it again. God help me, I've let them down.

They'd dug a shallow crawl pit under the fence. Now Sullivan lay flat on his belly in the dirt, just inside the barbed-wire fence around the camp. It was near dawn; a little blue was creeping into the sky's black. El-Mahud lay beside him, M16 under his hand.

"Now you're going to get a practical lesson in sentry removal," Sullivan had told him before they'd breached the fence.

Sullivan studied the sentry. The sentry was right-handed. Sullivan would approach from the left. He would wait till the sentry reached his about-face point, so that, when he turned, his left would be facing the river—the direction from which the greatest noise came. That would help cover the sound of Sullivan's approach.

But there were other considerations. And each one had to be covered. Because this was a critical moment in the mission. The whole thing could fall apart right here. He was near the heart of the enemy's power, toying with the fringe of its awareness. Mistakes made out on the perimeters could be covered up. But one shouting sentry here could end everything disastrously.

In his commando work as point man for the long-range reconnaissance patrols—patrols which in fact had as much to do with assassination and sabotage as with reconnaissance—Sullivan had learned that in taking out sentries the attacker sometimes had to deal with a kind of "sixth-sense" awareness, a projection on the part of the attacker and reception by the attacked. There was a mind-control technique for controlling the projection. The projection is real—it has been acknowledged by instructors in all branches of the armed services—but no one knows definitely what it is. Is it telepathy? More likely the killer is involuntarily creating tiny physical signals which are picked up by the target's subconscious, giving him an "uneasy" feeling.

The projection comes from the physical center of emotional sensations—the solar plexus.

Now, moving hunched over, sometimes on all fours, face blacked out, stripped down to camouflage clothing, a holstered machine pistol, and a knife, Sullivan silently approached the target. He was a tall, medium-heavy man with red hair and fair skin—probably an IRA terrorist.

The sentry, Sullivan had noticed, would walk to the end of his posting, pause there for a glance around—but never all the way around—and then slowly about-face to start back the opposite way.

Now the man was moving toward the north end of the compound, a few feet inside the fence, with his back to Sullivan. Sullivan moved in the same direction, but a little more rapidly, timing it so that he would catch up with the target just before he turned.

There were a few buildings off to the left, darkened, and beyond them the parade ground before the lodge. Behind the lodge was another fence stalked by another sentry. There was the porch sentry at the lodge, and one at each length of the rectangular fence. Sullivan knew their movements and had taken them into account.

The compound was ill-lit, and that worked in Sullivan's favor. The Blue Man kept it ill-lit—if a government copter happened to fly over, he didn't want it to see a military installation.

The critical moment was approaching. Sullivan was eight feet from the target . . . seven feet . . . six feet. The last four feet were the most dangerous. Optimum probability of sentry awareness. It was the tensest moment, and the effort at self-control brought sweat out on the back of Sullivan's neck. He was hearing the sounds of the night with super-human clarity. The insects sang in grating warning; the river was like a great animal breathing nervously, about to awake; faint creaks came from the barracks as the trainees tossed in their bunks. Sullivan's own breathing seemed impossibly loud in his ears. His heart banged in his chest, loud enough that surely the sentry would hear it. . . .

It was like stage fright. You never quite got over it. Seasoned warriors had to deal with the same nerve problems that racked amateurs. The difference was, they knew *how* to deal with them. Sullivan concentrated on directing a mental autosuggestion to the "emotional-projection" center at his solar plexus: *Freeze,* he told it. *Freeze. Ice. Feel nothing.* Then he expanded the freeze to encompass his entire body, a closed-in sensation, cocoonlike.

Sullivan moved lightly, willing his muscles to be relaxed, his limbs absorbing the vibrations of his own movement so that he made less noise. He moved fluidly, without definite starts or stops, all his motions circular.

The paradox was the necessity of moving softly, fluidly, almost gently—and then having to generate a high level of emotional ferocity suddenly, like pulling a trigger, when you came within striking . . .

Sullivan struck.

He cross-grabbed the red-haired sentry at a rear corner of his head and jerked him around and down at a forty-degree angle. He stepped under the direction of the man's fall, at the same moment clamping his left hand's fingers hard on the sentry's windpipe, cutting off the man's gasp of surprise. The cross-grab twist had exposed the sentry's neck; the carotid artery throbbed with life. In the moment of the sentry's greatest confusion, when he was falling back, Sullivan snapped his hand down from the man's head, drew his knife, raised it, and slashed—all in less than a second.

He held the man for a few moments as the artery pumped blood onto the thirsty dirt.

And then the man slumped. Sullivan held his windpipe for a few moments more, just to be sure, as the body spasmed in his arms.

Then he lowered him gently to the ground, easing him so that the weapon on his shoulder didn't clank.

The grab and slash had taken less than two seconds.

El Mahud ran up behind Sullivan, feet crunching in the dirt, breathing hard, clearly impressed. "It was a beautiful thing to see!" he hissed, too loudly. "You must remain with us, teach us, after—"

Sullivan made a slashing motion across his throat that meant *Cut it off!*

El-Mahud shut up.

They moved toward the shallow crawl space under the fence. Only the softness of the dirt there had made it possible to scoop out an entryway quick enough, while the sentry's back was turned. They'd lucked out on that too. Sullivan knew that luck was like cash—you spent it quicker than you knew. So: Caution. Care. Warning.

The other three Arabs came through the fence, all of them excited, grinning like kids. Sullivan made an emphatic gesture emphasizing: Silence!

All their compatriots had been housed in one barracks. There were only four men in that barracks who were not anti-Arafat Palestinians. They were Irishmen. They had to be regarded as enemies. Only members of El-Mahud's own sect, Sullivan insisted, could be trusted.

It would be a simple matter, theoretically, to kill those four men as they slept. To wake the others and tell them of Arafat's treachery. To lead them against the rest of the camp, using surprise to win out. There were eight sleeping Arabs in the barracks. With Sullivan's three, that made eleven. Against about thirty others. But it would be difficult for the Blue Man to mobilize the trainees against Sullivan's invasion force. Their allegiances were confused.

First, the other fence sentries had to be taken care of.

Sullivan knew their movement patterns. He had to work out how to hit each one without the others seeing it. He had to kill each one noiselessly, and quickly. And he had to do it alone.

He was not used to having to kill so many sentries alone. But the others with him couldn't be trusted to do it effectively, quietly.

So Sullivan did it.

One by one, he killed them.

He was tired, bone-tired, when he came to the fourth. It had been a grindingly ugly day, long and full of violence—the overt violence in the ravine, the covert violence of deception. He had marched his men for miles. He had killed and killed again.

The fatigue got to him, inevitably, and he made an error.

The fourth sentry was a hulking, brutish man with cauliflower ears and a flattened nose, skin like dough, eyes piggish-small. He carried a Skorpion SMG, which looked toylike against his bulk.

Sullivan crept up on the man—and three feet from him, he stepped on a crumpled piece of paper that had blown across the compound, almost as if the wind had decided to test Sullivan's alertness. He failed the test. He just didn't see it.

It made a small crackling noise under his feet. He froze.

The sentry turned, grinning. "I knew it," he said, chuckling, seeing Sullivan.

The sentry had made a mistake of his own, and it cost him.

The sentry thought of the camp as a training center—a tough one, where men were sometimes killed. But finally just a training camp. It didn't occur to him that he'd been given sentry duty for any real reason beyond mere training. He knew the camp was illegal, but they were a long way out in the woods. No feds out here. Nothing to worry about. Anyone breaking into the place would be a trainer, testing him. And he recognized this guy as an instructor.

This monstrous stupidity—the stupidity of thinking without flexibility—kept him from shouting a warning. He might have had help. But all he did was widen his grin, swing the Skorpion to point at Sullivan, and say, "Gotcha! Didn't get the jump on me!"

Sullivan relaxed and said, "Good. Not bad at all."

He came forward, smiling, as if to slap the sentry on the back. The sentry, proud, lowered his gun. Sullivan said, "Let's have a look at that weapon. You're supposed to keep it clean . . ."

"Sure." The sentry unstrapped it and handed it over. "How you gonna see down the barrel in the dark? You got a—"

Sullivan hit him hard between the eyes with the stock of the gun.

To his surprise, the sentry—as thick-skulled as he was beefy—didn't fall. He swayed, blinking, then made a grab for Sullivan's throat. And got it.

The sentry's hands were squeezing with a perfect equality of pressure, doing it the hard way—he wasn't concentrating the pressure on the windpipe, as Sullivan would have. But this way would kill too, given time.

Sullivan couldn't shoot the man. The noise would bring the camp down on him. He couldn't stab him—that'd make him scream.

But he had to do something. He was blacking out.

Sullivan braced on his left foot and kicked out hard with his right, swiveling his hips into the blow, sinking his boot into the hard man's breadbasket. The big man wheezed as all the air went out of him, and his grip loosened. Sullivan smashed the terrorist's arms aside, drew his knife, and stuck it to the hilt into the big man's right eye, driving the blade into his brain. The terrorist had no air in his lungs to scream with. He fell silently, dead on the instant.

Sullivan sagged to his knees, dizzy, weak with exhaustion.

Pull yourself together, he told himself. Fast.

He forced himself to stand. He found himself doubting the course he'd taken. Maybe he should have brought the men in by the gate, as if they were returning normally. But everyone knew he'd left with *six* men. Worse, he had to make the Palestinian terrorists feel that the whole camp was against them. If he brought them into a camp where they'd have a relatively friendly return, it could defuse all his work in turning them.

No. It had to be this way. To make them into his weapons.

This was another critical moment—when he was beginning to doubt himself. He was losing resolve, which meant losing the initiative, losing direction. Which would mean death.

He knew what he had to do. He had to get mad. He had to tap into that anger that gave him strength.

He closed his eyes for a moment. He saw Lily on the boat. Lily, waving to him. The bomb going off.

And Sullivan was trembling with the energy of renewed fury, with the determination of the vengeance-taker.

The Specialist had his strength back.

The barracks were up on concrete blocks. Under each one was an insulating crawl space. Sullivan had left the Arabs lying flat under their own barracks, where they were to wait for him. He returned to them now, and whispered terse instructions.

"No—we go with you!" El-Mahud said. Sullivan could not see his face in the darkness under the barracks.

"Keep your voice down! I'm going to kill the commander. That will paralyze resistance. You wait till I give you the signal!"

"When?"

"Soon. Very soon. Do not lose your courage."

"The others are afraid. We are defying those who—"

"You will be a hero to those who sent you here soon, when they learn that you uncovered the plot against your faction. Don't listen to this whimpering. And now, you are committed. We have come too far to stop."

And Sullivan moved off into the darkness.

15
Two Battlefronts in Two Wars

Pain brought Malta back to consciousness. Someone was kicking him, and the kicks made the bullet wound scream within itself. Malta opened his eyes and looked out through a pink haze at the motel room.

He was in a corner, propped against the wall. Dave Moran stood over him, grinning. That was who had been kicking him. "You're right, Bud," Moran said over his shoulder. "The damn nigger's still alive!"

"He's one tough ol' nigger."

"Well, he sure is that." Moran kicked Malta again. The pain lanced through him in blue fire.

Malta gritted his teeth to keep from giving them the satisfaction of hearing him cry out.

Angie cried out for him. He opened his eyes and saw her lying on the bed, tied at wrists and ankles with heavy-gauge rope. She was gagged—could only make inarticulate cries.

Foolishly Malta could only think—in French: Those ropes will hurt her skin. Nothing should touch her but silk.

Every time he took a breath, the blue fire flickered higher in him.

He could smell whiskey. The two rednecks had been getting drunk, maybe for hours. Probably arguing about what to do with the girl.

Malta's head lolled to one side and he saw some-one else was tied up. A stout man with a bruise on his forehead, tied up and gagged, unconscious. The motel manager. He'd heard the gunshot, had come to investigate, thinking some drunk was taking potshots at tin cans on the mantelpiece—and they'd had to put him on ice.

Moran hunkered down next to him. "I'm real glad you're awake, nigger. I'm real glad. We need to know something from you, see. Where your pal is. That homo nigger-sucking scar-faced buddy of yours with the cute tricks. Where is he?"

Malta's mouth was full of wood shavings and steel wool. But he licked his dry lips and forced out a few words slowly. Painfully.

"To give . . . directions . . . to find him . . . is very complicated . . . so I'd . . . have to write it down. But that wouldn't help you, because of course . . . you can't read."

Moran snarled and kicked him again. The pain came up and consumed him. It had brought him out of unconsciousness, but now it overwhelmed him and sent him back.

He fell over on his side. But just before his eyes closed, he saw the gun:

Even in the dark, it was easy to spot the out-perimeter sentry post. Against the backdrop of ashen-gray tree trunks, the three men sitting behind the camouflage blind were clearly visible. The blind was beside the trail that led into the woods from the camp's southern gate. Sullivan had passed it on his way out for training maneuvers. It was set up to be invisible from the trail.

Rolff and Snag squatted about forty feet from the machine-gun nest. Just near enough to make out the winking stars of three cigarettes glowing. The nest was between them and the trail. Down that trail a ways, Merlin and Birdwell waited with the mortar and the grenade launcher. The heavier equipment was too bulky to carry through the woods' underbrush. It would have to be brought to the trail. Which necessitated the removal of the nest guarding the camp's main approach.

The difficulty was in taking the nest out quietly. It was too close to the camp. Gunfire here would raise an alarm.

Snag sighed. It would have been so easy to take it out with a single grenade lob.

They had decided that it was best just two of them go in. That reduced the chances of someone making a noise that would put the sentries on their guard.

Rolff and Snag separated, moving to flank the nest.

Snag moved stealthily and smoothly, never doing the jerky zigzag from tree to tree, in short bursts, that some guerrillas favored. That swift, erratic movement caught the eye, in Snag's opinion. So he moved like a drop of mercury sliding across a tilted mirror.

He stopped within fifteen feet of them and crouched behind a thicket of waist-high ferns, listening.

"O'Hara, you're a lazy asshole."

"Yes," said an Oriental voice. "O'Hara, you had better go, you think, yes?"

"Fuck you, boys. I'll go when I'm ready. I'll get up and walk down the bloody trail and see nothing and nobody, and I'll circle the camp, and here I'll be again like ten thousand times before. So why bother, I'm asking."

"The Nine are all in camp tonight," said the first voice. "Those assholes have a way of making surprise inspections."

"They'll be meeting in the lodge for all the night, arguin' their money cuts. And reducing the cut we get. I say the hell with it."

Snag was moving in. The night air suddenly seemed chill on his neck. Slowly he reached down and slid the knife from its sheath.

Got to do this one right, make it up to Sullivan, he thought.

He was carrying a six-inch double-bladed boot knife, a Randall made from 440C stainless steel, with light, easy-grip handles. Designed for killing men.

The machine gun poked its dull gray muzzle from a cross-shaped hole in the camouflage blind. It looked like a Soviet weapon, though he couldn't be sure in the dim moonlight filtering through the trees—probably a 12.7mm M-1938.

There was a cartridge belt fed into the gun. It was ready to fire, bolt pulled back, waiting like a huge carnivorous insect on its tripod. Snag had to get it between that gun and its gunner, to make sure the man didn't fire a warning burst to alert the camp when they came under attack. That would be an awkward position for fighting.

For a moment he was afraid. And then he seemed to hear Merlin telling him: He got away.

Driven by shame and fury, he moved in.

"Okay," O'Hara was saying. "I'm going—"

A dark shape leaped from the stump of a log and landed full on O'Hara's back. The stumpy Irishman fell over, knocking down the machine-gunner. There was a tangle of men between the machine gun and the third man, who ran to reach it. The third man jerked up, stopping in his tracks, his shout muffled by the hand clamped over his mouth, as he writhed around, the cold steel blade twisting into his vitals from behind.

Rolff held him till he stopped thrashing, then looked up to see how Snag was doing. Snag and an Oriental were a confusion of thrashing limbs. Then the Oriental twisted free, jumped back, stood, and drew a pistol.

Rolff crouched, ready to spring at him, but it wasn't necessary. There was a sickening *chunk* sound, and the Oriental, bubbling, turned away. He walked two or three strides into the woods, plucking at the knife Snag had thrown into his torn throat, and then fell to twitch in the ferns.

Snag got to his feet, flicking leaves from his fatigues.

"Good throwing, for throwing in darkness," Rolff said grudgingly.

"Lucky hit," Snag admitted.

"Did you hear them say something about the Nine all being there in the lodge?" Rolff asked.

"Yeah. I wonder if Sullivan knows?"

"No," Rolff said, his tone brittle. "I don't think so."

"Shit!" Snag, running, led the way. Rolff was close on his heels.

Suddenly they were in a hurry.

"Hello," said Sullivan cheerfully, walking up the front steps of the lodge. He was casually wiping away night-fighter blacking with a turpentine rag as he came. "Is she in?"

The sentry on the lodge's porch looked confused. He was Portuguese, and sullen. "I thought you go on maneuvers?"

"Yeah, well, little problem, one of my boys broke his leg. Got to talk to Tora about it. Just got back. And . . . the colonel in?"

The Portuguese snorted. "Yes. But he sleeps with his eyes open."

Sullivan had stepped onto the porch, assuming an air of chumminess. He tried to project an image of himself as just another overworked, harried camp employee, one of the boys, like the Portuguese.

It seemed to work. The slender, dark-eyed man accepted a cigarette and relaxed, leaning back against the porch post, his Skorpion slack on its strap by his side.

Sullivan heard several male voices murmuring from within the lodge. The meeting-hall windows, on the first floor, were lit.

"Who's in there?" Sullivan asked, as if he didn't really care.

"The Nine. All come in today from around the world. Making a lot of talk about Blue Man. What a pain in the ass he is now, right? What to do. Why talk, I say. Shoot him."

Sullivan shrugged. "Some are still loyal. And there are important business contacts . . . Where is Tora?"

"Upstairs. Maybe with a man, maybe alone." He grinned. "I think she wait for you."

"I'd better not keep her waiting. . . . Something wrong?"

"Looked to me like . . . Where the sentries? I see them walk by over there every ten minutes or so, but it's been—"

Thuk: the sound Sullivan's pistol butt made on the back of the Portuguese's head. Sullivan caught the man as he slumped, and dragged him to the door. He held him with one arm, reached with his free hand to open the door, pushed it inward. He dragged the man into the unoccupied hallway and stashed the body in a closet.

He appropriated the Skorpion, checking to see that the small submachine gun was ready to fire.

He went quickly to the stairs, on the way passing

the closed door behind which the top nine planners in the Blue Man's international-terrorism ring talked of betrayal and business practicality.

Would Tora be in there with them?

He stopped short at the top of the stairs, forcing self-control on himself, when she came out of her room. She was dressed in gray fatigues. Going to the meeting.

They stared at each other for a moment. "You are back early," she said.

He nodded. "Will they stick with him? Or will they kill him?" he asked, nodding toward the door at the bottom of the stairs.

"They've decided to stand behind him, if I can get him cleaned up. They need him to deal with Carlos. Carlos is a major customer—Carlos and Qaddafi. Both of them will deal only with Father."

"Where *is* the colonel?"

"My room. I tried to get him in shape to talk to them." She shook her head. Suddenly she asked, "Where's Bronnard?"

"He tried to kill me."

"Then . . . he's dead."

There was fear in her eyes when she looked at him.

"Tora . . . I need your help. I need to decode something in the files. It's important. It's important to *you*." It was, in fact. Because if it turned out that she'd had some direct part in arranging Lily's death, he would have to kill her. If she hadn't been directly involved, he could spare her. "I can't explain at the moment. But if you'll trust me . . ."

"I haven't time."

"Then show me the code-book key. I'll do it myself."

She hesitated. "It would take you a long time. I've got the process memorized, I can translate for you quickly. If you'll wait, I—"

He took her hands in his. "I can't wait."

He squeezed her hands. The touch was a promise. She shivered, and said, "All right, but quickly."

She led the way down the upper hall to the office door. She took a key from a pocket, unlocked it, and they went inside. She went to a corner, moved a wastepaper basket, and then a section of floor, a camouflaged trap beneath it. She reached into the secret compartment under the floorboards and brought out a black book about the size of a lady's address book. "It's all here," she said. "You know cryptography?"

He nodded.

She went to the files and unlocked them, pressing the button sequence for the override in the combination lock.

There was a click, and the file was unlocked.

It was only three feet high. Everything in it could be transferred to a backpack. And for the first time, she seemed to notice that Sullivan was wearing one. An empty one.

She stared at it. "What—?" she began.

He silenced her with a kiss.

She closed her eyes to savor it. Then he stepped back and let her have it. He hit her across the side of the neck, the edge of his hand angling precisely to chop the nerve there. She sagged, out cold. He caught her before she hit the floor.

"This way," he said, laying her out on the rug behind the desk, "you'll have a chance."

He unstrapped the backpack and went to the file, began to fill the pack with file folders.

He finished in five minutes, and shouldered the pack. He turned to the door, just as it was opening.

The blue-skull tattoo on Thatcher's face was more pronounced than ever. It was as if it took on life even as Thatcher wasted away.

Thatcher's eyes were glassy, and he swayed. But he had a machine pistol in his hand, and he still knew how to use it.

He raised it and fired.

16
The Bloodbath and the Sacrificed

The machine pistol flamed, racketing with ear-cracking noise in the small room. Thatcher sprayed it to the right and left like a child playing with a water hose, careless of accuracy.

Sullivan dived behind the desk, unslinging the Skorpion, as 9mm slugs smacked into the walls just over his head, cratering the wood, explosively shattering the plaster idol of multiarmed Vishnu in the windowsill, blasting the window to tinkling shards, rattling holes into the metal file cabinet—the cabinet exploded, the booby trap inside it triggered by a stray bullet. Flame erupted where the filing cabinet had been as the shock wave blew the Blue Man back into the hallway. He lay outside the door, stunned. Flames crackled up the walls, looking like hungry Oriental dragons as they consumed the old wooden beams.

"Son of a *bitch*. You just never know," Sullivan muttered, climbing out from under the overturned desk. Tora lay beside it, unhurt.

He moved through the roiling smoke to the door, flattening to one side of it. The smoke stung his eyes, and the crackling boards sizzled with burning pitch.

Sullivan waited. He heard shouts from the room below, and automatic rifle fire from another building. That would mean that El-Mahud had taken the sound of an explosion from the lodge as Sullivan's signal. Sullivan had told them to listen for a blast—but this wasn't the explosion he'd intended. He'd planned to blow up the whole building.

Thatcher came into the room, staggering blindly, firing random bursts. Sullivan caught him from behind in a half-nelson, disarmed him, and dragged him out through the door. The Blue Man struggled in Sullivan's grip for a few moments and then seemed to accept it as an unavoidable part of the dream he was in. "I know who you are," he said, speaking to Sullivan's fist. "You're the hand of Jack Sullivan. The man who said he was Stark. I saw it tonight in a vision. The opium cleared the lie away, the illusion vanished, and I saw the truth. Jack Sullivan. I recognized him from a photo—three years ago. A file snap. The Specialist. And you—you're the hand of the Specialist, come to kill us all. I knew, I knew. But she didn't believe me. She was blinded."

Sullivan dragged Thatcher down the hall to the top of the stairs. He held him in front of him, a shield, and with his free hand fired the Skorpion at the doorway below. The men crowding through the doorway tried to back up, and got in one another's way. One of them fired a .45 automatic at Sullivan, splintering the banister post. Sullivan's Skorpion chewed holes across the doorframe and through three male torsos—it was happening fast, the men were just a blur for Sullivan—and then across the doorframe on the opposite side. He fired another burst in the contrary direction, cutting an X across the doorway. Men screamed and fell shaking atop one another; a pool of red spread from the door.

Sullivan dragged the limp, babbling Colonel Thatcher down the steps, the man's boots banging as he came.

Sullivan fired short bursts at the door, four rounds,

six rounds, never too many, conserving his clip, knowing he wouldn't have an easy chance to put in a fresh one.

Someone appeared in the doorway during a lull in the firing, just when Sullivan reached the bottom step, and brought a pistol up to target Sullivan. But the man paused, gaping in indecision, seeing the Blue Man in the way, and Sullivan shot him in the head with a short burst at two-yard range, making the skull fly apart in irregular red chunks, spattering the door behind him with scarlet.

Sullivan's clip ran out. He dropped the Skorpion, snatched a grenade from his belt, pulled the pin, and flattening with Thatcher beside the door, tossed it backhand into the meeting hall. There were screams, shouts of, "Kick it back out!" and then a concussive roar that shook the building.

Sullivan dragged Thatcher past the smoke-spewing doorway and down the hall, out onto the front porch.

There was a firefight going on, raging between two barracks. El-Mahud had roused his friends, they'd broken into their barracks armory, and after killing those in their quarters who weren't with them, they'd gone after the other trainees and staff, hoping to catch them confused. The thing had happened too soon—and now, like the fire consuming the lodge at his back, it was raging out of control.

Gunfire lit up the night in strobe bursts, lizard tongues of muzzle flash snapped back and forth between the squat buildings.

And then the mortars came down.

Merlin and Rolff were walking mortar shells across the compound, in the pattern Sullivan had worked out for them, erupting outbuildings, storage sheds, munitions—triggering more explosions and sending fountains of wood fragments and dust into the air. In the space of ten minutes the various human booby traps Sullivan had set up had all been triggered; a small holocaust was let loose to storm unpredictably through the camp.

The Blue Man was laughing. "It's beautiful!" he cackled. "Look at it!"

"Sullivan!" Someone was shouting at him from behind. "Turn around and take it!"

Sullivan turned, jerking the Blue Man around with him.

Tora.

She stood in the doorway, shaking, her clothing charred, her hair half singed away, boils along her right cheek, her neck.

"I—" Sullivan began.

There was a gun in her hand, a pistol she'd taken from one of the dead in the hallway. It spoke, and interrupted Sullivan.

She fired spasmodically, seeing only Sullivan through her pain and anger, wanting to kill the man who'd betrayed her.

The bullet caught her father in the forehead and splashed his brains on Sullivan's chest.

"Father!" she screamed.

Sullivan dropped the body and leaped to one side. Her next shot caught him as he went, shattering his left leg at the shin. Sullivan hit the porch floor, rolled, gritting his teeth at the pain in his leg. He lost his grip on the submachine gun.

He rolled off the porch as she came out after him.

Sullivan still couldn't bring himself to shoot her down.

She stood on the porch looking down at him. And then she did a strange little dance, jerking, as red circles the size of quarters appeared on her neck and cheeks. The red circles gushed blood as she fell back against the wall.

El-Mahud came to stand beside Sullivan, his M16 smoking. "I save your life, yes?"

Sullivan reached out, jerked the Arab's ankle so he fell heavily on his back. The Specialist drew a knife from his boot sheath and stuck it directly into the young Arab's heart.

He looked up to see Morgan and two others coming at him, running between the smoking craters across the compound.

Morgan had a look of pure fury on his face, and Sullivan knew he'd somehow found out that it had all been a setup. Probably they'd captured one of the Arabs, who'd told them what had happened in the woods.

Sullivan got to his good leg, pulling himself up by using El-Mahud's M16 as a crutch. He was feeling weak from blood loss, and the sky seemed to rotate slowly overhead; the ground was turning in the opposite direction beneath him.

He felt sick, and he couldn't quite flush away the vision of Tora dancing under the M16's gunfire. He wanted to go and lie down somewhere.

But Morgan and two Spaniards with nasty white grins were thirty feet away and coming at him with assault rifles. They had fixed bayonets. They wanted the pleasure of carving him up.

Sullivan leaned his weight on the unhurt leg and raised the rifle. It didn't feel quite right under his fingers. His fingers had become things of soft clay.

He struggled grimly to get the gun cocked and into position.

He knew he wasn't going to make it in time.

Snag.

Snag was there, running up from the right, positioning himself firmly between Sullivan and the three oncoming men, dropping to one knee, firing his M16. Morgan and another man shouted and

172

stumbled, then fell, clawing dirt, as the slugs tore into them. The third man squeezed off a sharp burst that caught Snag full in the belly, six shots at twenty feet, making his guts so much confetti.

Snag scream and fell back. Sullivan had the rifle in position, and a spurt of adrenaline brought the strength back to his limbs. He snapped off three shots at Snag's killer. The man fell, spinning, shot through the face.

Sullivan hobbled to Snag and bent beside him.

A strange silence had come to the camp.

The mortar bombardment had ceased; the gunfire had lulled. Now he heard only the crackle of the flames in the buildings behind him. The compound was well-lit by fire from three buildings, throwing dancing figures of light and shadow across the open spaces. Bodies lay sprawled in the dirt here and there; smoke drifted over the wreckage.

Sullivan cradled Snag's head in his arms. "You're hurt bad, Snag. You got to lie still till we can—"

"Forget it," Snag croaked. "I'm fucked good. Gone. I . . . gotta tell you . . . I blew it. I let that government agent get . . . get away. I'm sorry . . . Jack . . ."

"Sorry? Man, you just saved my life! Listen, you . . . you did a good job, Snag. You're no drunk Indian. You're a *soldier*."

Snag smiled, and closed his eyes. Closed them for good. Sullivan eased Snag's jacket off him and covered his face with it.

Then, fingers moving mechanically, he made a tourniquet from a rifle strap and stanched the blood flow on his wounded leg.

Birdwell came trotting heavily up through the smoke, coughing and swearing. "Hey, Sullivan, there's three more of them. Of the Nine!"

Sullivan looked up. "Where?"

"We saw 'em go out a window when the shooting

173

started. They're getting aboard a chopper in the clearing. They came in a chopper about three hours ago—"

"Get down!" Sullivan shouted.

Birdwell flattened on the dirt beside him.

Sullivan pointed. There were six armed men across the compound, between two of the burning buildings, standing in a group. They appeared to be arguing. Two of them were pointing toward Sullivan. Sullivan thought he recognized one of them as training staff.

The six men started across the mortar-pocked compound toward them.

"Where are Merlin and Rolff?" Sullivan asked.

"They used up the mortars so they went on a mop-up. Listen, you seen Tora?"

"She . . ." The agonized look on Birdwell's face brought Sullivan up short. He was saved from having to tell him.

Saved by several tons of flying killing machine.

It was a Bell HH-1K chopper, with a Lycoming T53-L13 engine, a big mother, with a top speed of one-sixty and a range of over three hundred miles. It was designed, originally, for air-sea rescue missions, which gave it a long-haul capacity perfect for the trip into the country to the camp.

It had been modified. In the metal frame of the open side door was a 7.62mm Minigun—a machine gun capable of firing four thousand rounds per minute. The gun could be unscrewed from its mounting in case of an FAA inspection.

The FAA officials would've turned white, seeing what happened next.

The chopper cut low over the burning buildings, the flames licking at the fuselage, the blades angled into the mushrooming black smoke, whipping it into shreds—red muzzle flash spat bullets so fast all the detonations merged into one unbroken purr of gunfire. The dirt leaped and danced under the impact of the spitting tumblers, catching the six trainees coming at Sullivan in a hail of death.

Two strafing passes, the thundering chopper whipping up the dust and mixing it with smoke, and the six camp men were so much chopped meat, lifeless, sprawled, limbs jumping under the impact of the now unnecessary slugs.

Sullivan, watching in disgust, realized that the chopper was strafing the camp's own men because the three who'd survived from the ruling council knew the game was up—they were eliminating anyone who could identify them as having been a part of it. Killing whatever moved in the camp.

He turned to warn Birdwell to get under cover—and saw he was gone.

Sullivan got to his knees, and, eyes burning, peered through the smoke.

Birdwell was climbing the steps of the burning lodge. The porch hadn't yet been consumed by the striated red and black fires, though waves of heat rolled out from the burning building, and timbers collapsed, crashing the roof in on itself with a fountain of sparks. The porch roof was burning merrily.

Shielding his eyes against the heat, bathed in yellow light, Birdwell cried out—he'd seen Tora's body on the porch.

"Birdwell, dammit—!" Sullivan shouted. "Get the fuck away from . . ."

He broke off, staring. Birdwell had picked up Tora in his arms. The limp, shattered body streamed blood to soak his clothes. Birdwell was sobbing. He carried the body to the porch steps but didn't descend. He simply stood there on the porch, weeping. The monster he'd loved was dead in his arms.

And then the copter roared down on them, its lights flashing, search beams swiveling over the shattered earth, hungry for new victims, its blades making a hurricane as it approached.

Sullivan was moving on elbows toward the partial cover of a mortar-shell crater. He rolled into it just as the Minigun whipped 7.62 slugs into the dirt around him, the rounds burying themselves in the dirt inches from his head.

The copter spotted Birdwell, still bawling on the porch steps and oblivious of anything but his grief.

The Minigun ripped into the porch roof, which collapsed under the combined attrition of flames and heavy-gauge gunfire, burying Birdwell in a burning hell of glowing timbers.

The copter came back for another pass, and Sullivan knew they'd seen him.

Pounding bootsteps—Sullivan brought the M16 around, and froze his finger on the trigger just in time to keep from blowing Merlin and Rolff in half.

They jumped down into the crater with him.

"Sullivan, we—" Merlin began.

"Shut up!" Sullivan shouted. "And give me that goddamn grenade launcher!"

The copter was angling down, thundering as it came, fanning the fires in the buildings, searching for Sullivan, intent on its own mission of vengeance.

Merlin gave him the grenade launcher, which he fixed onto the muzzle of the M16. When he fired a shot, the expanding gas following the bullet would launch the grenade.

The copter slowed, rotating to give its door gunner a better shot at the three men. The Minigun stitched a line of rounds up to the crater, Rolff and Merlin returning fire with their SMG's. Their rounds ricocheted harmlessly from the armored chopper.

But Sullivan, forcing himself to get to one knee, fighting dizziness, gauging the distance and the probable trajectory of the grenade . . .

Fired.

There was a moment of uncertainty.

Bullets whipped the dirt up around them.

And then the copter exploded, became a fireball forty feet away, lighting up the surrounding woods.

The frame broke in two and fell to the center of the compound. Shrapnel sang through the air, sizzling lethally around them. Merlin took three fragments in the right pectoral; Rolff took one in the thigh; Sullivan felt one gouge a new scar across his cheek.

Then the camp was quiet except for the occasional rumble of a collapsing building and the voracious sounds of fire eating old wood.

"Merlin . . ." Sullivan said. He slid back down into the crater, blood-loss weakness catching up with him.

Merlin threw an arm over Sullivan and helped him to stand. Rolff noticed Snag's body. He picked it up in his arms and followed Sullivan and Merlin to the trail that led to the river.

They knew they had to find a quick way out. Because Knickian had gotten away—and he'd be bringing an invading army of feds back with him.

To the world, if it knew what had gone on here, Sullivan would be a hero. But to the feds he was engaged in criminal interference with their activities.

They had reached the river, had just finished burying Snag under a cairn of stones, when they heard the first of the DIA copters approaching, cutting through the gray light of dawn, looking for someone to blame.

17
White Water, White Slaughter

"Stay where you are!" boomed the voice from the bullhorn on the copter. *"You are under arrest!"*

The pain was chewing on Sullivan's leg like a rabid animal. He could feel broken bone-ends grinding together. It must have showed on his face, because Merlin said, "Hey, Jack, I've got some morphine in the medical kit . . ."

Sullivan was tempted. But he shook his head. "No, I'll need my head clear till we get out of their reach."

Rolff was untying the black rubber raft that the Blue Man had left here as a quick escape option. He pushed it down the pebbly bank to the edge of the rushing white water, then slung its lead rope over a branch projecting from a riverside tree trunk. He pushed the raft into the water with one hand and a shoulder; with the other he held on to the rope. The river grabbed the raft and tried to wrench it away. Rolff hung on bitterly, grimacing, using the pulley leverage of the branch against the tug of the furious current. "Get in!" he shouted at them. Merlin helped Sullivan to the raft, then climbed in himself. Rolff followed, still holding on to the rope. The raft bucked like a mustang in the rodeo chute, eager to get under way on the white water of the Rogue River.

Once they were in position and braced, Rolff let go. The river caught them up and spun them away.

The copter chopped by only thirty feet overhead, looking like a UFO, all lights and bulk, hovering just above the trees, as the bullhorn warned, *"Stop or we'll have to shoot!"*

"*Stop?*" Merlin yelled over the thunder of the waters. "Like we could stop if we wanted to!"

It was true—they were almost completely in the river's power. He could use the oars only to steer a little, to try to avoid the rocks.

The Rogue is a serious sportsman's river. There is no casual boating on it. That would be like attempting hang-gliding in a tornado.

The river was fast, twisting—and narrow. Massive saw-toothed black rocks seemed to fling themselves at the raft. The big raft rebounded like a pinball and spun sickeningly fast through whirlpools. The icy water soaked them in mist and spray. The tree flew past when they came to the narrow stretches, the river sometimes taking them as fast as fifty mph.

The river thundered and roared, lifted them up on the brinks of small waterfalls, and smacked them down.

Another time Sullivan might have enjoyed the ride. Now, weak from blood loss and pain, fighting shock, he struggled to hold on, his fingers quivering with the cold, the heat of living sucked out of him. He slipped into a partial delirium, believing he was falling head over heels through interstellar space, doomed to fall endlessly in the eternal cold.

And then he felt warmth on his face, and a touch on his arm.

"Jack?" The voice sounded distant. "You okay?"

He opened his eyes. It was Merlin standing over him. Sullivan looked around, blinking. They were in the shallows, far downriver from the camp, at one of the rare places where the river slows and widens for a while.

"There's a trailer park not far from here, Jack," Merlin said. "Rolff went to see if there might be a doctor there. I'm gonna give you a shot of morphine . . ."

"The . . . the copters?"

"They went over looking for us a few minutes ago. Rolff got us in under the trees. They missed us. Come on, it's too cold here. The water's freezing my feet off. Let's go."

Sullivan struggled through waves of pain, each one like a furious ocean breaker trying to knock him down. After a while he was up and out of the raft, leaning on Merlin, hopping on his good leg up the bank. When they got to the bank, Merlin dug in a canvas pouch, removed a prefixed morphine syrette, and jabbed it into Sullivan's arm. The pain ebbed, and a warm darkness took him away on yet another river, this one wide and slow and very, very deep.

It was two days before he was clearheaded enough to sit up in bed and wonder where they'd taken him. It was a hotel room. He could hear city noises outside the window. He looked under the bedsheet— his wounded leg was in a cast.

There was a hanger for a plasma bottle beside the bed, and a bandage on his arm where he'd had intravenous. The hotel room was dull green; above the bureau across from him there was a decorator painting of a family of bears splashing in a creek.

"Christ," Sullivan muttered. His leg throbbed and burned.

And then all the questions boiled up in him.

Where were the files? Where were Merlin and Rolff? Had the police found them? Where was Malta?

180

He felt under his pillow, by reflex, for a gun. There was nothing there but the crisp white sheet.

The door opened, and a scowling black woman with badly straightened hair came in, dressed in an RN's white. "What the hell you think you doing? Lay on back down there!"

"Where am I?" Sullivan asked. "Who . . . ?" He broke off, seeing Merlin at the door, a sad smile on his gaunt face. He knew, seeing that look, that something had happened.

Something bad.

"I tol' you lie on down—"

"It's okay," Merlin said, coming into the room. "He's a big boy. I'd better talk to him alone."

She took her scowl out of the room, and Merlin closed the door behind her and came to sit on the edge of the bed.

"The files," Sullivan said.

"They're okay. They got wet, but they're intact and readable."

"The cops?"

"Nobody's onto us so far as we know. We had to bribe a lot of people to get your leg taken care of without having to answer a lot of questions about a gunshot wound. We got you a doctor and a private nurse here. We figured it wouldn't be safe in a hospital. This is a hotel in a town called Bend."

"You were wounded."

"Little shrapnel. Nothing. Rolff's okay too."

"Then . . . what?"

Merlin looked at the floor. "It's Malta."

Sullivan stared at him.

"He's dead. Gunshot wound in the chest. Those rednecks you told us about . . . I'm sorry, Jack. I know he was a buddy of yours. He was something else, that guy."

Sullivan suddenly felt deeply tired. It's war, he

told himself. People get killed in war. War against terrorism's the same. Or worse.

But no matter how hard he tried, he couldn't keep from blaming himself. Tora. Snag. Malta.

"We'll get the sons of bitches," Sullivan said softly.

"No need. I'll let Angie tell you—"

"Who?"

"You'll see." Merlin went to the door, opened it, and a plump, busty, apple-cheeked blond walked in. She wore a long black dress.

"The barmaid!" Sullivan blurted.

"Not anymore," she said, sitting in a chair beside the bed. "I quit. Moved out of the Riverbend." Her voice broke. She swallowed hard, making an effort to keep from crying. She took a deep breath and went on, "Malta told me a lot about you. I want you to know what happened. . . . I was in his place with him. We'd been seeing each other for a few days. He . . . I guess I was in love with him. He spoke so nicely. He was a sweet guy, but real strong too. I guess I . . . Anyway, that Moran and Bud Hauser came around, crazy drunk . . ."

She told him the story in bits and pieces, getting it out painfully.

". . . So when he insulted them, implied they were too dumb to read, they kicked him, knocked him out again. Then they . . . they went to the bed, and started to do things to me . . ."

Sullivan saw the bruises now, imperfectly hidden under her makeup.

She continued, ". . . and I guess I screamed. Then I heard a funny sound. It was somebody clearing his throat—a real theatrical sort of way. Like, *Ahem*, you know? And I looked past them—that Hauser was taking his pants down—and I saw Malta standing up. He was leaning back against the wall, and his chest was all bloody, and he looked real wobbly.

182

But he was standing up. I don't know how he did it, with a bullet through the right lung. But he stood there shaking his head, saying, 'Excuse me, gentlemen. I wonder if I might have a word with you.' He had a gun in his hand. I guess when he woke up, he found it on the floor. His gun. They were drunk, and it was under the bed. They missed it. So then . . ." She paused, swallowing. "So then he said . . . Well, what he said was like out of a movie, but, you knew him, you know that when he says it, it's for real. He said: 'Gentlemen, you have abused and insulted a lady. I must ask you for satisfaction. Kindly reach for your weapons.' His voice was all raspy and weak, you know—but he said it, clear as a bell. And that Moran, he grabbed up a gun and turned and got ready to shoot, and . . . and Malta shot him right between the eyes. Then he shot Hauser—he shot him clean through the heart. They fell over dead, just like that. And Malta . . . he said my name. Then he fell over, and he was dead too."

She burst into tears.

Sullivan turned his face to the wall.

After she had gone and Sullivan had eaten, Merlin returned with a box full of papers and a small black book. The files and the code book.

"You sure you want to do this now?" Merlin asked. "Maybe you ought to rest, man. You lost a lot of—"

"Bring it here!" Sullivan snapped. "The mission's not over yet."

18

Three Very Special Bullets

"Seems to me," Merlin said, "a lot depends on Al-Fahad's not knowing what happened at the camp. Okay, you met this guy Dutchmont at the camp, and he left on this Al-Fahad assignment. But if Dutchmont heard what happened at the camp, the whole thing might be off. I mean, it was the Blue Man who sent him out to help Al-Fahad. Once the Blue Man's dead, Dutchmont's risking his ass for nothing, because it's the Blue Man who would pay him."

"They won't know what happened yet. With luck. There's a news blackout," Sullivan explained. "The feds aren't ready to talk about it to the press till they get a story that doesn't make them look silly. We got everyone at the camp—or they got one another. If anyone lived, wounded, the feds got them locked up. The radio was in the office—that went up in flames. How *could* Dutchmont know?"

They were in a rented Buick, parked outside a brownstone in New York city, one week after the bloodbath in the camp. Rolff sat in the backseat, smoking. A drizzling rain hung a gray curtain across the dull urban scene. A few people hunched under umbrellas passed with typical New York haste.

"You sure this Dutchmont will remember you?"

"I'm sure. I listened to him beef about the Blue

Man for an hour and a half. Dutchmont was the only assassination operative who went out while I was there. He told me he was going to New York to set up this hit with Al-Fahad, and he was stupidly informative about the details. Trying to get in good with me after he saw I was close with the boss's daughter. He'll check the place out the day before the . . ." Sullivan cut off, peering through the misted windshield. He sat beside Merlin, who was the driver. He nodded. "That's him. We timed it right. He's going in for a final look at the target."

The man Sullivan identified as Dutchmont was a tall blond, about thirty-five, his face tanned, his expression surprisingly friendly. He was always friendly-looking, Sullivan supposed. Even when he was twisting a knife in your gut.

Dutchmont wore a blue trench coat and a blue fedora. He carried no umbrella. He walked past the residence of the ambassador from Israel more slowly than the other pedestrians, looking it over casually, as if curious about the official-looking seal on the door, the security guard on the porch.

He smiled at the guard, and the guard smiled back.

He walked on and turned the corner. Merlin eased the Buick sedan from its slot and followed.

Dutchmont got into a waiting car, a VW Bug. Someone dark-skinned, wearing a suit, was driving it.

Merlin followed at a discreet distance, until they turned in at the parking garage for the Hilton.

"The Hilton," Merlin remarked. "These dedicated strugglers for the people sure live high."

Merlin pulled up across the street. Rolff got out to find out what room Dutchmont went to.

Sullivan sat back to think it out.

*   *   *

Five years earlier, Jack Sullivan had been in Israel helping a friend set up a training center for antiterrorist commandos. His friend Moshe, of the Israeli Mossad, had gone home one day to find his wife and family dead, blown up by a terrorist's bomb. A radical Palestinian faction called the Palestinian Rights Struggle took credit, claiming to have made an example by killing the family of one of their movement's greatest enemies. Moshe Shmuel himself would be next, they promised.

The Mossad went into high gear to look for the PRS, but Sullivan was convinced they were following the wrong leads. He went after the PRS himself, and found out that the leader of the group was one Al-Fahad, an Arab who had one particularity. He never wore a burnoose. Despite his denunciations of the West, he always wore a three-piece suit of the best British tweed. Even in hot weather. He was rarely seen, never traced . . . until Sullivan traced him through a British detective who interrogated nearly every tailor in London.

Sullivan found Al-Fahad and his cadre in a London apartment, building a bomb. There were ten of them in there. When Sullivan was through, there was only one left alive. Al-Fahad.

Al-Fahad escaped, and Sullivan never caught up with him.

The Arab hadn't seen the man who'd killed nine of the men closest to him. But he'd heard the rumor: the Specialist was responsible.

Al-Fahad had gone to the Blue Man, paid him to find Sullivan and to kill him. The Blue Man had sent Rusty Spike to do the job. Spike had planted the bomb on the boat—the bomb that killed Sullivan's Lily. Sullivan had gotten to Spike, and he'd gotten to the Blue Man. But Al-Fahad was the man who was really responsible. And now it was his turn.

Dutchmont recognized Sullivan immediately, and opened the door, grinning with relief. "Had me worried. I thought you were the feds," he said after Sullivan had come in. Sullivan leaned on a crutch, hobbled on a cast. "Busted that in the woods," he explained.

The suite was painfully modern, its decor all stripped to clean, streamlined simplicity; the paintings on the wall were the sort of abstracts painters churn out to match furniture colors. Al-Fahad sat at the bar, doing something very un-Muslim: drinking a highball.

Sullivan nodded congenially at him and shook Dutchmont's hand. "How's it working out?"

"Pretty well." Dutchmont couldn't hide his nervousness, despite his easy veneer of friendliness. "You . . . uh . . . ?"

"Yeah. The Blue Man says . . ." He paused, glanced at Al-Fahad. The immaculately dressed terrorist gazed evenly at Sullivan, looking strangely relaxed. Sullivan went on. "He says you have to shift operations base. Now. Tonight. There's a security problem."

"Who is this man?" asked Al-Fahad in a voice like warm petroleum.

"Name's Stark. He's close with the Brown Angel."

Tora: the Brown Angel.

"What's the security problem?" Dutchmont asked, smiling, swallowing, afraid it might be him. You never knew whom the Blue Man might capriciously single out, the way he was behaving lately.

"Some nut hot for the Blue Man's ass. Seems his

old lady kicked and he's blaming us." Sullivan smiled.

Dutchmont smiled back.

Al-Fahad scowled. "It is not the time for relocation. It is too late."

Sullivan shrugged. "You paid the Blue Man for someone to do some reconnaissance and background for you. The Blue Man is involved. It's not safe for him if it's not safe for you. He says it's not safe for you. You don't risk the Blue Man. You come with me. We'll build the device out at a place I know. I'll help. I'll give you a hell of an explosion."

"This place is too far from the city," the Arab complained.

It was a deserted farmhouse in Westchester County. It was half-overgrown by vines, and part of the roof had fallen in. "We cannot stay in such a . . . a broken-down place."

"I thought you revolutionary terrorists were tough," Sullivan said, opening the gate.

Reluctantly the Arab walked across the wet lawn and up to the porch. The clouds had cleared; they could see by moonlight that the front door was slightly ajar.

A faint spill of light came through the open door.

Dutchmont and Al-Fahad went ahead. Sullivan waited till they'd gone into the center of the room before following.

The room was lit by candles.

There were seventy-five candles arranged about the room, and near each candle was a photograph, upright. Candles against the marble of the old fireplace's mantel; candles flickering on the window-sills and on the cracked wooden table. Candles with framed photographs, all alike.

Seventy-five photos of one woman.

"Who is she?" Dutchmont asked huskily, his hand snaking toward the gun inside his coat.

"Her name was Lily," Sullivan said. "She was someone who mattered."

Al-Fahad had turned to stare at him with widening eyes. "Who are you?"

"Me?" Sullivan just stood there as Dutchmont drew his gun. Sullivan made no move to go for his own, though he had a Heckler and Koch self-loading pistol, 9mm parabellum, snugged against his ribs. Sullivan leaned his left side on his crutch. His right arm hung limply. "I'm the Specialist," Sullivan said.

Dutchmont raised the gun and aimed—and jerked around, spun, and fell, his chest smashed open by a quick burst from Rolff's Uzi. Rolff stepped into the room from the door leading into the kitchen. Merlin was waiting on the road with another car.

Al-Fahad was trembling, but he made no move to run or to fight. He stared at Sullivan. "I knew you were coming. I knew the bomb must have missed you. I knew . . ."

Sullivan drew the police pistol. "There are just three bullets in this," he said. He took aim. "The first one's for Snag." He fired, and the terrorist's right kneecap exploded. The man fell onto his side, wailing.

"The second is for Malta."

He put a bullet through the squealing terrorist's belly, where it would hurt him, but not kill him.

"And this one's for Lily." He put a bullet through the terrorist's brain, and holstered the gun.

Sullivan hobbled to the mantel, took a candle and a photograph, one in each hand. He set the photo afire and used the burning snapshot to fire the peeling wallpaper.

The wallpaper went up quickly, and the building began to burn.

Sullivan and Rolff went silently out into the damp night, and let the past burn behind them.

The Specialist Questionnaire

Win A Free Gift! Fill out this questionnaire and mail it today. All entries must be received by June 30, 1984. A drawing will be held in the New American Library offices in New York City on July 30, 1984. 100 winners will be randomly selected and sent a gift.

1. Book title:_____

   Book #:_____

2. Using the scale below, how would you rate this book on the following features? Please write in one rating from 0-10 for each feature in the spaces provided.

POOR		NOT SO GOOD		AVERAGE			GOOD		EXCEL- LENT	
0	1	2	3	4	5	6	7	8	9	10

RATING

Overall opinion of book...................... _____
Plot/Story .... _____
Setting/Location............................. _____
Writing style .... _____
Dialogue .... _____
Suspense..................................... _____
Conclusion/ending............................ _____
Character development .... _____
Hero .... _____
Scene on front cover......................... _____
Colors of front cover........................ _____
Back cover story outline..................... _____
First page excerpts.......................... _____

3. How likely are you to buy another title in The Specialist series? (Circle one number on the scale below.)

DEFI- NITELY NOT BUY	PROB- ABLY NOT BUY			NOT SURE			PROB- ABLY BUY		DEFI- NITELY BUY	
0	1	2	3	4	5	6	7	8	9	10

4. Listed below are various Action Adventure lines. Rate only those you have read using the 0-10 scale below.

POOR		NOT SO GOOD		AVERAGE			GOOD		EXCELLENT	
0	1	2	3	4	5	6	7	8	9	10

RATING

Able Team................................. _____
Death Merchant .... _____
Destroyer................................. _____
Dirty Harry............................... _____
Mack Bolan (Executioner)............... _____
Penetrator .... _____
Phoenix Force............................ _____
Specialist .... _____
Survivalist .... _____
_____ .... _____
_____ .... _____

5. Where do you usually buy your books (check one or more):
( ) Bookstore   ( ) Discount Store
( ) Supermarket   ( ) Department Store
( ) Variety Store   ( ) Other:_____
( ) Dug Store

6. What are the names of two of your favorite magazines?
1) _____
2) _____

7. What is your age? _____   Sex: ( ) Male
                                        ( ) Female

8. Marital Status: Education:
( ) Single   ( ) Grammar school or less
( ) Married   ( ) Some high school
( ) Divorced   ( ) H. S. graduate
( ) Separated   ( ) 2 yrs. college
( ) Widowed   ( ) 4 yrs. college

If you would like to participate in future research projects, please complete the following:

PRINT NAME:_____

ADDRESS:_____

CITY:_____STATE_____ZIP_____

PHONE: (   )_____

Thank you. Please send to: New American Library, Action Adventure Research Dept., 1633 Broadway, New York, New York 10019.